S0-AHY-679

Two Scars Against One

Books by LaJoyce Martin

The Bent-Winged Series:
    To Love a Bent-Winged Angel
    Love's Mended Wings
    Love's Golden Wings
    When Love Filled the Gap
    To Love a Runaway
    A Single Worry
    Two Scars Against One

Pioneer Romance:
    Love's Velvet Chains
    So Swift the Storm
    The Wooden Heart
    Heart-Shaped Pieces

Western:
    The Other Side of Jordan
    To Even the Score

Nonfiction:
    Mother Eve's Garden Club

Two Scars Against One

. . . .

by LaJoyce Martin

Two Scars Against One

by LaJoyce Martin

©1994, Word Aflame Press
  Hazelwood, MO 63042-2299

Cover Design by Tim Agnew

Cover Art by Art Kirchoff

All scripture quotations in this book are from the King James Version of the Bible unless otherwise identified. All rights reserved. No portion of this publication may be reproduced, stored in an electronic system, or transmitted in any form or by any means, electronic, mechanical, photocopy, recording or otherwise, without the prior permission of Word Aflame Press. Brief quotations may be used in literary reviews.

Printed in the United States of America.

Printed by

Library of Congress Cataloging-in-Publication Data

Martin, LaJoyce, 1937-
    Two scars against one / by LaJoyce Martin.
        p.   cm.
    ISBN 1-56722-025-8   ::
    1. Frontier and pioneer life—Texas—Fiction. 2. Mothers and sons—Texas—Fiction. 3. Women pioneers—Texas—Fiction.
I. Title.
PS3563.A72486T86   1994
813'.54—dc20   94-3763
                                                                CIP

Dedicated to:

My only brother, Bobby

CHAPTER 1

The Telegram

To Martha Harris, wedlock meant what it said.

"When ya wed, ya lock arms t'gether an' tread life's trail to th' finish," she told her nine children. "Be th' path strewed with stickers or be it reefed with roses."

According to Martha, one locked in with one's spouse forever and threw away the key. "Love can't add. It's always one, no more." It was as simple as that.

"An' jist because ya lock horns in a fuss is no cause to split th' blanket," she said. "Why, ifn I hadn't been pad-locked to yore paw by that preacher man, I'd'a undone with many a tiff. Even on days when we splatted like a churn an' a dasher, we couldn't manage one without th' other."

When the children were younger, they reacted to her "mama sermons" in variegated ways. Sally giggled. Chester nodded. Matthew sat unblinking. Sarah feigned boredom. Alan fidgeted. Dessie looked out the window toward the woodshed. The others usually managed to escape somehow.

"Marriage is a *vow* to God, stouter than a 'pledge allegiance to th' flag," she would expostulate. "An' to break a vow is a pure-out way of tellin' a lie." Sometimes she would add her most fearsome verse of Scripture: *All liars shall have their part in the lake of fire.* At other times she would forget and leave it off.

So when Chester's marriage came to an end, she almost did too. That such an atrocity could happen to one of her own was too awful to contemplate. She claimed the blow hit her so hard it knocked her "ten years onward taward yon graveyard."

"An' it's a good thang Henry's a'ready turned to dust," she declared. "He couldn't'a stood it." She threw up both hands in an exasperated half prayer. "God love his soul! He died an' left th' worstest of th' worryin' up to me. Worry keeps me busier than a barefoot boy standin' on a anthill!"

Sally, who lived in her mother's back yard, tried to console her. It didn't work.

"But I thought," reasoned Martha, "that when I got Alan married off, my worries would be over. That was th' last of my brood a-solo. An' now *th' worst thang in th' world has happened!* Sally-girl, it's worser'n *death!*" Out of her ample apron pocket came the cup towel to sop up the tears.

Sally spent the next few months patiently trying to explain away Martha's endless "whys." When she chopped down one, another grew in its place.

"Our Chester was bound to be good to her."

"Yes, Mama."

"I'm satisfied that he loved her."

"Yes, Mama."

"An' he never neglected her fer his work."

"No, Mama."

"Solomon said to ever'thang there's a season. I say to ever'thang there's a *reason*. Now, Sally-girl, if I could jist figger a reason—"

"Mama, you can't lay the blame—"

"I ain't tryin' to find a patch to plant no blame in, Sally. Puttin' down seeds o' blame is a bad thang to do. They grow all weedish without waterin', then ever'thang gits stickery. I'm jist tryin' to make some sense in my mind of th' whole thang before it insanes me."

Martha finally worked herself into such a fret that Sally feared for her mother's health. That's when she decided to go to Chester's office in the nearby village of Walnut Springs to have a talk with him.

Chester was busy when she arrived, attending to a nasty cut on a toddler's head. When he finished cleaning the injury and pulling the skin together, he plastered the wound with the thin membrane from an eggshell. "An old wives' remedy," he said with a chuckle, "but it will keep the gash from leaving a scar. I don't like *scars*."

Sally watched as Chester lifted the child from the table and put him into his mother's waiting arms. How could such large hands be so tender?

When they were alone, he turned to Sally with brother-ly intuition. "What's wrong, Sally?"

"It's Mama, Chester. You and I need to have a talk."

Chester walked to the door and hung out the "Closed" sign. "So we won't be disturbed," he explained. "Now tell me about it."

"Ever since you came back here, Mama has been bent

out of shape over the . . . the end of your marriage."

"You're not telling me anything I don't already know, Sally."

"But I thought as time went on, it would get better. It hasn't. It's getting worse."

"Now you know why I refused to move in with Mama. It would have been miserable for me—and for her. I don't want her to see or feel my grief on a daily basis. So I moved here, to the closest town, to be near her. I knew she would be crushed by the failure of my marriage. I would do anything to spare her the hurt. That's why I kept it a secret for two years."

"You . . . ? Two years?"

"Yes. Candice left me two years before I said a word about it to any of you. Can you imagine how it felt to come to the family reunions those two years and *pretend?* I didn't even live where you thought I did."

"I'm sorry, Chester. I didn't know. . . ."

"Then I began to feel I was living a lie, hiding the truth from my family."

"What *is* the truth, Chester? That's what I've come to ask. I would never pry for myself, but Mama must have some answers, or we'll soon be calling the asylum or the mortician."

"I don't want to put Candice in a bad light. How did Mama always put it? To 'lay her name on people's tongues.' "

"Please just give me the barest of facts then. For Mama."

"You'll have to understand it from the start for it to make sense." He pulled his chair around to face her, and she noticed that the pain in his eyes had intensified.

Why wouldn't any woman love this handsome man: tanned, muscular, and broad of shoulder? He'd won the race with his twin brother, Alan, as seventh of Martha's children. The president that term, Chester Alan Arthur, had made a fan of Martha, and she named her newborn sons for him, adding Arthur the next year. Henry called the three his "President's boys." He claimed Chester was no bigger than "a drowned rat" at birth but that he made up for lost time before "the grass put out" in the spring.

In their growing-up years, Chester had been Sally's favorite brother, taking her side against any foe, real or imagined. He had turned out big-hearted, good-natured, and fine-principled. What had happened to shatter his marriage?

"Tell me only what you feel I need to know."

"You were still a lass in pinafores when I went to work with the street crew in Fort Worth, sister. I liked my job and marriage was the furthest thing from my mind. I allowed that would come in its own God-appointed time."

Sally took a deep breath and leaned back in her chair; she'd been afraid he wouldn't talk.

"I burned my foot with some hot tar, and the boss insisted I see Dr. Randolph Bond who happened to be Candice's stepfather. She was in the infirmary that day and made a return appointment for me. And for such a minor injury!

"The appointments never ended. She was warm and friendly; I was away from home and lonely. Her attention was flattering. Candice claimed it was love at first sight for her."

"I can understand how she fell *in* love, but how did she fall *out?*"

"I'm getting there. The telling won't rush. Her mother, Hortense Bond, found out about her daughter's interest in me, and the fat was in the fire. She said no child of hers would marry a common laborer; she'd invested too much in the girl for her to waste herself on a peon."

"Why, the snob!"

"Well, yes, I guess you could call her that and be justified. She forbade Candice to see me, but Candice made a way. The more her mother fought the friendship, the more Candice strove to nurture it. I rather admired her spunk. Here was a gal who had enough grit and gumption to cross class lines.

"Hortense shipped men in from every port to snag Candice's attention, but she spurned them all for me. You can see how that would make a fellow feel.

"Candice was quite a bit younger than I, but she knew her way around—I didn't. I had lived on the farm all my life, a country boy. The city, the luxury . . . it intoxicated me.

"But I tried to keep one foot on the ground. I pointed out all the reasons why we should not marry. First and foremost, her mother and stepfather objected. Then there were our backgrounds, painted on different canvases.

"When her stepfather, Dr. Bond, saw that Candice had her heart set on me and had marriage in her mind, he came up with a suggestion that he felt would solve the dilemma. He and Candice saw the potential of a doctor in me. And I have them to thank for that.

"Dr. Bond offered to finance me through medical school if I would pay him back in services for one year following my graduation. Then if I didn't like the profession, he said, I wouldn't be bound to it. It sounded fair enough—and Candice's mother seemed mollified.

"The next semester, I enrolled in college. Candice thought we should go ahead and get married before Hortense changed her mind again—"

Sally shifted. "Mama always felt a little hurt that none of the Harris family got to attend the wedding."

"I was disappointed that none of you came—or ever mentioned the reason why."

"We weren't invited."

"You . . . *what?*"

"We didn't even know the date."

"Candice told me that her mother had taken care of the invitations to my family." He dropped his eyes. "And she took care of it all right, didn't she? She saw to it that none of you attended. I'm sorry, Sally. It's all clear now. Hortense didn't *want* any of my family there. She didn't want anyone to know—" He shook his head as if to clear away some unseen web lodged there. "Dear Lord, forgive me! I was so blind!" He clasped his hands together in a pitiful prayer.

"Mama doesn't hold it against you." Sally reached out to touch his sagging shoulder.

"That precious matriarch! Grudges are beyond her when it comes to one of her children. Where did I leave off? Oh, yes. Dr. Bond sent his stepson, Candice's brother, to medical school, too. We both worked for Dr. Bond, and of the two of us, he considered me the better doctor. That didn't set well with Hortense.

"All the while, though, Hortense was bragging to all her highbrow friends about her 'doctor son-in-law' in an effort to convince *herself* that Candice had married well. She decided I should have my own practice and my own hospital.

"I found my joy in working with children and wanted to go into that line of work. When I saved a child, I felt I had saved a *whole* life. Besides, I love children. But Hortense disliked children, declaring them a waste of my time. She wanted me to be a heart surgeon. That's where the fame and money hid, she said. I cared for neither fame nor fortune.

"In her spare time, Hortense was trying to break down my home-taught principles. She ridiculed me for not joining society's merry-go-round of dancing, drinking, and card playing. I was quiet and courteous in my refusal; she interpreted that as weakness and tried the harder to de-religion me.

"I didn't realize how much effect she was having on my spirit until I came home for the family reunion the year Alan married. He was perceptive enough to see that my soul was rusting out. I had become disillusioned with Candice's formal church—which was nothing more than a social gathering—and had stopped going altogether.

"Then the night I thought we were going to lose Nellie's baby, I made some promises to God. . . ."

"I remember."

"I decided that no one had the responsibility of my soul but me. And nothing or nobody was worth losing it. I went back to Fort Worth a different man . . . and the real trouble started. Until then, Hortense thought she had me jelling into her mold just right."

"Candice called two or three times during that year's reunion—"

"Wanting me to come home and procure some downtown property for a Harris Hospital. I got the property—

or rather, Hortense got it—and the hospital was built. I don't know what its status is today."

"None of us will ever forget that reunion! Of course, we weren't surprised that Candice wasn't with you. She seemed uncomfortable the one time she did come."

"She didn't understand, Sally." The tone of his voice defended her.

"I recall that she was offended by our 'homemade prayers' as she called them: at the table, at bedtime, at the cemetery. She insisted that God should have prayers read from a book written by someone who had a proper command of words instead of the anything-and-everything we wished to tell Him. She thought we were being disrespectful."

"That's the way she had been taught. I tried to lead her gently to our simple way of worshiping God. . . ." Love honed his words. "But—" his voice broke, "I didn't reckon with her mother having such an influence on her."

"So with your new dedication to God, Candice asked you to leave?"

"No, it was she who left. Hortense convinced her that I was a religious zealot bent on pulling the rungs from her social ladder. Candice was too beautiful, too popular, and too young to become a 'puritan,' her mother maintained. She was missing all the fun of the theater crowd. She was meant for something more glamorous. The stage, modeling, opera . . .

"The woman seemed to have some uncanny power over her daughter. Candice acted differently after she had been with her mother. Abstract. . . .

"They left while I was at work one day. Candice left me a note telling me that our marriage had been a mistake.

She had other things she wished to do with her life."

"Do you think there was . . . someone else?"

"No!" Chester's teeth clamped down on the word then turned it loose. "Candice had very high morals."

"And you haven't heard from her?"

"Not a word. I stayed there all that winter, hoping she would change her mind and come back. It was a long, miserable season! How I missed her !"

"Do you have any contact with Candice's stepfather, Dr. Bond?"

"Dr. Bond is dead. I read about his death in a medical journal. It seems he had gone out of state to escort an indigent patient to the hospital and died of a heart seizure before he got back. The article eulogized him. He was a good man; I owe him a lot."

"And so you moved here," supplied Sally.

"After an interim. I . . . searched for Candice for several months, but I never found her. I did love that beautiful lady, Sally. Devotedly. There was so much *good* in her; she was a generous, compassionate person." A tear splashed onto Chester's shoe.

Sally sat frozen, trying to decide how to spoon-feed this knowledge to her mother slowly so that Martha wouldn't choke on it. "I'm . . . I'm glad you chose Walnut Springs to set up your practice. We . . . we needed you. We like having you close by."

"My reasons for coming here are personal. Ever since our brother, Robert, was killed in the horse accident, I've wanted to doctor here in The Springs. That was before you were born. I was quite small myself, but I remember it well. Then Mama lost her first grandbaby to the flux. . . ."

"Are you satisfied here, Chester?"

Chester shook his head. "I *thought* I was. But lately, I've begun to feel restless, as if I'm supposed to be somewhere else or doing something else."

"You are needing companionship, brother. If I have it figured right, Candice has been gone for about five years now. You need someone to fill her place."

"No one could fill her place."

"Couldn't you file for a divorce on charges of abandonment?"

"No, I couldn't file for a divorce. You know that. Mama *would* die. She doesn't believe in divorce. Remember what she used to say about wedlock? *You throw away the key.*"

"But in your case—"

"I couldn't do it, Sally." He waved one hand as if to shoo away the thought. "Wherever Candice is, she still belongs to me. I'm not sure I could *ever* love anyone else. I vowed I'd be true to her until death parts us. And Candice is still alive."

"Do you think she'll be back?"

"As long as Hortense lives, I have no reason to hope."

"I'm sure you've made it a matter of prayer?"

"Yes, with nothing but a heaven of brass."

"It doesn't seem fair, Chester."

"Life isn't always fair, Sally. No one knows that better than a doctor. But I can be thankful there were no children, as dearly as I would love to have a child of my own. To think that I'll never have a little girl to call me daddy . . . or a son. . . ." He dropped into a crevice of silence, and Sally knew the painful discourse had ended.

She reached for her handbag. "Thank you for telling me. I'll go along before Mama puts out a search warrant for me."

"Now you know why I hate *scars*, Sally. My heart feels like one giant scar—"

A sharp rap on the door cut his sentence in half. "Can't they see the sign?" he grumbled.

The knocking continued, becoming more urgent.

"Whoever it is must know that you are here."

"It must be an emergency." With a quick jerk, Chester pulled the door open.

"I'm sorry to bother you on your day off, doctor." Sally heard a man's husky voice. "And especially for such a message. We have a telegram for you. Is there someone with you?"

"My sister is here."

"Then I'll bid you God's grace and comfort." The bearer of the message hurried away.

"How strange!" Sally mused. "God's grace and comfort . . . What made him say that?"

Chester's eyes scanned the telegram, and he caught the edge of the table for support.

"Is it . . . *bad* news, Chester?"

He traced a slow circle around his mouth with a trembling hand. "Y-yes. It's from my mother-in-law."

"From Hortense? Why would she—?"

"Candice is dead."

CHAPTER 2

The Client

"**C**ome on out to Mama's, Chester." Sally insisted on riding the twelve miles to Martha's with him.

"No," Chester said. "I have a few things to do yet. You go on. Mama will be worried about you if you wait for me. I'll be all right." He hurried her out, wanting to be by himself.

After Sally left, he stared at the telegram, mockingly devoid of details, for a long while. He gripped his temples to block out the sight of Candice lying cold and stiff in a coffin, fighting thoughts that threshed about in a whirlpool of regret. If he'd had a little more time . . . If he, instead of Hortense, could have been the sculptor, the potter . . .

When they first married, he had seen little portholes of light: the woman Candice could be, the bulb below the surface. He had convinced himself that Candice would someday emerge into a lovely wife and companion.

Scenes kept shifting in his head. At the end of his

medical training, Candice had thrown her arms about him in a grip of desperation. "Let's get away," she begged. "Far, far away so that we can live our own lives."

It wouldn't be honest, he explained, to back out on his agreement with Dr. Bond to repay the education loan with a year's service. A year wouldn't be long; then they would relocate.

Candice was crestfallen. "Mother will never give me a moment's rest as long as I'm here. Did you know, Chester, that she doesn't ever want us to have children? And I want *lots* of them. I love babies. I'm going to name our first little girl Chessica just for you!"

The year that had seemed so short had been too long. Slowly, imperceptibly, like a boa constrictor squeezing the breath from its victim, Hortense had fashioned her daughter into a flighty, shallow shell of the woman Chester had wed. When the year ended, Hortense "surprised" them with a lavishly furnished apartment near her. Dr. Bond set Chester up with a practice of his own. And Candice no longer mentioned leaving.

He'd told himself that someday Hortense would lose her hold on Candice; that was his last hope. And today that hope had turned into another scar on his heart.

Chester stuffed the telegram into his pocket and removed the "Closed" sign from the door. He had planned to close the clinic for the rest of the day, but he needed the work to dilute the scalding emotions and to hold memory at bay. He must not sit here and let the past torment him; it was gone.

He longed for a client—anybody, any diversion—to put his day back into perspective, to occupy his hands and heart . . . and his mind. Chester's clinic seldom lacked for business, and he didn't have long to wait. A well-dressed woman with raven black hair and intense, violet eyes opened the door, making the bell jangle noisily.

"Dr. Harris!" Her eyes smiled with the rest of her face.

"Yes?"

"You don't remember me?"

"The face, but not the name. I'm sorry."

"I'm Molly. Granddaughter of one of your mother's old neighbors, Myrt. We had a sing at Granny's the year your twin brother, Alan, married the schoolteacher. I believe it was the year your wife didn't get to make the trip with you—"

Chester cut her off with a nod. "I do miss your grandmother at church since . . . she departed. She played me to sleep many a time when I was a boy."

"I'm sure Granny is plaguing the angels to let her play the big pipe organ in heaven at this very minute." Molly grinned. "I hope they know she can't read notes."

"It's a comfort to know where she is." Chester avoided her eyes. "Some people aren't so fortunate."

"Yes, we're blessed in many ways. Among our blessings is a doctor in The Springs. Of course, no one could have prolonged Granny's life. Her lifetime guarantee expired years ago." She maneuvered the subject back to Chester. "And is your family well?"

"Mama is fine. I, well, I just lost my wife." Chester wanted to bite his tongue for blurting it out. For a doctor to impose his personal problems on a client wasn't ethical.

"Just . . . today?"

"I got the message today."

"Oh—" She stumbled for words. "How sorry I am, doctor! How may I help out? With the funeral meal and all, I mean. Will the parson at Brazos Point be in charge of the arrangements? Your wife will be buried in the Harris plot, will she not?"

The moment was awkward. How could he explain without explaining too much? "I . . . I'm . . . that is . . . she was away when she died, and I haven't much information yet. I just received a telegram."

"Then you'll be going . . . and you were getting ready to close."

"Were you seeking medical assistance?"

"Yes, but nothing that can't wait until you return. I don't wish to burden you further on this sad day. My husband and I are moving out to Granny's place. I was in need of a tonic for our youngest son. Oh, wait! You'll remember him! His name is Oscar Adams."

The blank expression answered for Chester. "No, I'm afraid . . ."

"During your reunion that year, a family was stranded at the river: a couple whose daughter had died and left four orphaned youngsters. They gave the two younger children, a tiny baby and a mute girl, to your sister-in-law, Nellie Gibson—"

"Susan and Billy."

"The two older boys, Rufus and Oscar, went on with the grandparents."

"I didn't meet them, but Alan told me about them."

"Those two boys belonged to my husband, Eli Adams. We married that same year and began our search for them. And what a chase they gave us! We combed the country for the better part of a year. When we did locate them, the grandmother had died and the children were near starvation, along with their pitiful grandfather.

"To take them from their grandpa would have finished the poor fellow off, and Eli didn't have the heart to do that. Earl Taylor really loved those grandsons. So we moved in with him and took care of them all—plus a one-eyed mule and some molting chickens. Old Mr. Taylor joined his wife shortly thereafter.

"Eli has made a responsible father and a good husband. Our sons will love Granny's place, and I'm ever so happy to have a family doctor!

"For so many years, Dr. Harris, I didn't realize what really mattered in life. Why, I couldn't love those boys more if they were my own! And I do want to take good care of them. I hope that Granny can look down from heaven and see what a good mother and wife I'm making!"

"Do the boys remember Susan and Billy?"

"Oh, yes! When I promised that they would get to see them again, they cried with joy!"

"William and Nellie will be happy, too. They live in Cleburne now. William owns a blacksmith shop there. They come to see Mama often. Please be seated, and I'll mix you a tonic for Oscar."

"Oh no, Doctor! I've already been rude enough. I wouldn't think of imposing upon your time on a day when you've suffered such a personal loss—"

Chester disappeared into the medicine storeroom before she could finish her sentence. He was glad to find a use for his hands and his mind. He returned with a corked brown bottle and waved away the money she tried to offer. "Children are my weakness," he said. "I should listen to my heart and go to a city hospital where I can work with them exclusively."

"Please don't, Dr. Harris. You can't run out on us now

that we're just getting here!"

When Molly left, Chester's restlessness intensified manyfold. He paced the length of the office, back and forth, back and forth, like a caged animal seeking escape. *The notice of Candice's death caused this feeling.* He stopped. *No, the unrest is too familiar, too old to be born today.* How far back did it reach? He couldn't remember.

He started his agitated walk again. He stopped again. He couldn't stay here and pace all night. He'd wear the floor (or his feet) threadbare.

He had to find out something . . . something to quench this torment.

Chester lifted the telephone's ear piece and gave the operator Hortense's number in Fort Worth. His hands were clammy, his mouth dry. A maid answered the ring and said that Mrs. Bond was not at home. And no, she knew nothing of the death of Mrs. Bond's daughter. That must have happened before she was hired on. No, she hadn't heard anyone mention it. And yes, she would be glad to take a message and ask Mrs. Bond to return his call. Might she ask who was calling? And no, she didn't have any idea when the call would be returned.

He called Candice's brother. James Sharp no longer had an affiliation with the Bond family, he was informed. And good day. Click.

In the back closet there was a wreath left by the last entrepreneur. Perhaps he should put it on the door.

The drugstore calendar on the wall showed the date as April 7. It was Candice's birthday; she would have been twenty-six.

He locked the office and set out for the home place.

CHAPTER 3

A Visit Home

April was unwinding. Grackles circled and called, dark silhouettes painted against the clear sky. Bluebonnets swarmed the fields with their thick, spendthrift blooms.

The bluebonnets reminded Chester of Effie, a girl cousin who had lived with them. Though crippled, she was a spunky girl. With her beautiful lisp, she would say, "Ch-Chester, I p-prayed a p-prayer and God a-answered my p-prayer just as p-pretty as a b-bluebonnet!" The perennials were her "favoritest of all God's flowers," and she liked them "morether" than the others.

Even then, he had wished he could be a doctor to help children like Effie. Suppose God *meant* for him to work in a hospital where there were many, many children like Effie? Children with defects . . . children no one else wanted to be bothered with . . .

The telegram crackled in his vest pocket like static on a radio: *Candice-is-dead. Candice-is-dead.* He had offered sympathy on countless occasions, but taking it would be harder. The smothery mothering from Martha would have to be faced. She meant well.

The home place, wrapped in a glow of boyhood recollections, came into sight. There was the bald casing suspended from a hemp rope for a swing, the barn with its malodorous loft, the lightning abused tree—all of which had provided him with his share of pleasures and accidents.

The house itself was large, the most imposing of the clump of farm houses that made up the tiny community. The cool evening justified the whiff of smoke that tailed up from the rock chimney. The picket fence, the eaves, and the porch columns owed their thanks for a fresh coat of paint to Sally's husband.

It would be hard to wind life's reel back to the "old poor house" as they all called their dilapidated shack that "sprawled like a tumblin' woodpile." Effie, an unsuspecting heiress to a large inheritance, had the new home built for them before she took flight on her golden wings.

Chester was glad he had sent Sally on ahead. She would fill Martha in on the history of his rocky marriage. Martha would take Chester's side, right or wrong. Prejudice blinded her to her children's shortcomings the moment each of them entered the world. After this storm blew over—and it would—the healing would begin. . . .

Martha heard the heel of Chester's boot on the porch step and reached the front door before he did. "My Chester!" she crooned. "When a child o' mine troubles, I trouble double! Come on in an' eat a good home-cooked meal. I made cracklin' cornbread jist fer you. A full stummick that's warm around food helps other hurtin' places."

He hugged her, half wishing that he could be a little boy again, waist high, his arms wrapped about her middle as far as they would reach, and that his mother's arms could hold his world together as they once did. Oh, to be able to reverse the gears of life and start over! But as Papa used to say, "Life has only one direction and that's straight ahead on with a straight head."

"Sally didn't give me no sidedish facts on th' tragedy that took Candice, Chester," Martha barged right in. "Wuz it a illness or a happenstance?"

"I don't know, Mama."

"Why didn't they call fer you?"

"I don't know that, either."

"Wuz they still off a-traipsin'?"

Chester bunched his big shoulders.

"Well, where hied th' telegram from?"

Chester fished the yellow page from his pocket. "It was sent from Fort Worth, but that tells me nothing. Someone could have sent it for Hortense. I have no way of knowing when or where Candice died or where she has been laid to rest."

"Couldn't you call on th' horn?"

"I tried. All I could learn—from one of the servants—is that Hortense is away. I don't expect her to return my call."

Martha stared at the message with its pasted-on lines. Her faded gray eyes took on a calculating look as hardset as overcooked molasses. "Somethin' don't smell right, Chester. Mayhap Candice ain't really dead."

"Under no other circumstances would Hortense have contacted me. She would have no reason to notify me if it wasn't true. She disregarded me completely while

Candice was alive."

"Why would she contact you now?"

"I was still Candice's legal husband."

"Exactly! Yore still th' woman's legal son-in-law, and that's why she wants you ta believe yer wife is dead. Cause ifn you believe it, she'll be shed o' you ferever, see? Th' woman plans that her daughter have nuthin' ta do with you, ner you with her, ferevermore."

"No, I'm sure—"

"Sally told me undecorated about th' woman's feelin' tawards you, Chester. They ain't gold plated."

"But a fictitious death notice? No one would stoop that low! Not even Hortense. That would be *cruel*."

"Cruel is braided into them kind's nature."

"The message is genuine, Mama. I have no doubts. The hardest part is knowing that I'll probably live out my life not knowing a shard more about what happened than I know today."

"Ain't you got a house? Er land? Er th' hospital?"

"No. Everything was in Dr. Bond's name. Since I had no money, he financed everything. When he died, the property would have gone to his wife."

"How convenient-like."

"I wouldn't want it without Candice anyway."

Chester thought Martha had dropped the subject when she made her abrupt announcement: "I was a-thinkin', Chester, that I might like t' go an' spend a coupla days with William an' Nellie in Cleburne. Sarah's Hank could take me. You could stay here an' Sally could cook fer you. Me an' you both needs time ta git our minds washed out an' hung up ta dry. I've been through a bad worry fer a long, long spell now. I want ta git thangs settled so's we can all unworry."

She conveniently swept the telegram off into a drawer out of his sight. "Jist you try to fergit an' git yer mind smoothed out again."

Her surprises never failed to catch Chester off guard. This whim, especially, seemed out of character for her. But it was a harmless idea and would spare him a few hours of "poor-Chestering."

"I think that would be a good outing for you, Mama," he agreed. "Go and have a good time. Worry never solved anything."

"Nellie writ that William got hisself one o' them new-fangled horseless carriages. I onct thought I'd be as scared to ride on one as I would a long-horned bull, but I'm thankin' I might ask William ta take me fer a little ride-around." Her plotting smile shot right past Chester. Her prattle, he thought, was her way of comforting him, this conversation offered as a purgative for his bleeding spirit.

How many years had it been since his mother had left her home to visit one of her children? Or had she ever? The evening, the condolences, everything was turning out better than he had hoped. He was glad he'd made the visit.

Chester would have been appalled if he could have peeled off the layers of Martha's plans and got a glimpse of her motives. In fact, he would have demanded that she not make the proposed trip at all.

"Mama? Going on an out-of-town visit?" Sally raised her eyebrows in a crooked arch when Chester told her. "Is she *all right*, Chester?"

"It will do her good, Sally." Chester nodded. "Encourage it. Help her pack!"

CHAPTER 4

Woman to Woman

Martha threw her cotton gown into the old leprous suitcase while no one was looking. To her, any nightdress was immodest regardless of its long sleeves or full length. Sally caught her with her black pan hat, outdated by twenty years, in her hand.

"You won't need that thing, Mama!" she sputtered. "William won't expect you to wear a hat."

Martha's chin went out. "You jist never know what I might need, Sally-girl. This here is *my* trip, an' I'll take what I well please." Any further words from Sally were wasted. In went the hat to be crushed with the rest of her belongings.

When she was all packed, she asked Sally to ring up Sarah's husband on the "horn" to come and get her. Hank did a good job of camouflaging his astonishment at Martha's impromptu trip.

William was pleased to see her, albeit troubled. "Is something wrong, Mama?" he asked, taking her suitcase.

"Never felt better, William," she said, "ner more in th' Lord's will."

"Making your maiden voyage at age seventy-two?" he teased.

"A bizness trip, William." She whispered behind her hand so that Hank couldn't hear. "A bizness trip."

Five-year-old Billy greeted her with open curiosity. He'd been to Grandmam's many times, but Grandmam had never been to his house. This was a rare treat. "You'll play with me, Grandmam?" he asked.

"Likely I won't have no time to play, Billy." She drew herself up to her full stature. "You see, this is a bizness trip."

"Oh." The child seemed disappointed. "What's bizness, Grandmam?"

Martha turned the question aside, giving her attention to Susan. "My dear," she smiled, "you will soon see yore brothers!"

"Oscar and Rufus? *Really?*"

"Fer a fact."

"They're my *half* brothers, Grandmam." Martha noticed how grown-up she had become. "My mother called them my brothers-on-the-halves. Where did you find them?"

"Their papa and mama, Eli and Molly, er movin' in close to me where my old neighbor lady used to live."

"I thought Oscar and Rufus went to live with Grandma and Grandpa Taylor."

"They did, fer a fact. But yore Gran'pa an' Gram'ma Taylor took a new address up in the sky—an' their own pa found them jist in time to give 'um a home."

"Oh, I'm *glad*. And won't they be *amazed* when they

32

see how Uncle Chester fixed me so I can *talk?*" Susan loved emphasizing words when she talked. "When I was little and they pulled my pigtails, I wanted so *badly* to yell bad words at them! Maybe it's a good thing I *couldn't* talk." She folded her hands in her lap. "I'm *so* anxious to see them again!"

That evening, with the prayers said and the children dismissed for the night, Martha pulled her cane-bottom chair between William and Nellie. "Now I need ta tell you my bizness fer comin'," she said. "None o' them back home know. They thank I'm jist on a friendly visit, but they should'a knowed better. Have ever I friendly visited any of you before?"

William laughed. "Not that I can remember."

"Chester got hisself a telegram this week that Candice is dead—"

Nellie's hands flew to her face. "Oh, no, Mama!"

"I have th' telegram right here in my purse fer proof." She rummaged through her handbag, found it, and handed it to William.

"Chester was always the best of us . . . the kindest," William shook his head in disbelief. "And his heartaches have been the worst. Some things are hard to understand."

"Yes. He was th' *givin'est* of all my children. Unselfish to a fault. He'd give away his lunch at school an' do without hisself ifn some child looked hungry. He was a softie fer little thangs an' hurtin' thangs."

"And now he is outhurting us all. I've often wondered why the road to heaven seems to be graded smooth for some and full of washouts for others," William commented.

"Well, that gets me ta why I've come this eighteen mile," Martha said, squaring her stooped shoulders. "I want ta help his hurtin' ifn I can. You see, his mother-in-law balongs ta th' devil hisself. You can tell by th' short an' mean telegram that she's a-slappin him with. No details. No whens er wheres er hows. He's a-sufferin' a wonderment what happened to his Candice. An' she'll never tell him nary another word from now to doomsday. But *I* plan to go myself to Fort Worth an' find out some facts. I plan to settle up some of th' wonderments in Chester's achin', breakin' heart. An' I'm trustin' you to take me to Fort Worth in yore horseless, William Harris."

"Why, Mama—"

"Don't why-Mama me! How else would I git there? Ifn you don't take me, then I'll *walk*."

"The vinegar of a mother!" exclaimed William. "Of course I'll take you. Does Chester know about this?"

"No!" A pinpoint of fear showed in her eyes. "An' he *mustn't.*"

"All the better. If you find out nothing, we have lost nothing."

"Chester wouldn't like me pryin'. But seein' as they won't tell *him* nuthin', I plan to learn some partic'lars by hook er crook!"

"Chester might not be happy about it, but if you find out something that will salve his mind, he'll be glad you went."

"With yore horseless, we could git there in a day, couldn't we?"

"In my automobile, we can be there in an hour, Mama. It's only thirty miles to Fort Worth."

"Ooooo! Not so fast, William!"

The next morning found William and Martha jouncing over the brick streets of the city looking for the person listed on the telegram. "Chester may have helped lay this very boulevard," William said.

Martha's face might have been etched in stone, so inscrutable was her expression, leaving William to ponder if her first ride in a car would be remembered with pain or pleasure. When the vehicle listed to one side or the other, she grabbed for her hat. The hat, William supposed, made her feel dressed up and equal to any modern dame, when indeed it branded her as out of step and unfashionable as a powdered wig.

William stopped to inquire only once.

"Anyone in town could have told you where Dr. Bond's mansion is," the gregarious informant said. "Of course, the great doctor is deceased, but his widow lives there yet. She still has plenty of money and plenty of influence. She lives there in the mansion with her daughter. There's been some scandalous dispute with the son over the settlement of Dr. Bond's affairs. It was shamefully broadcast in the newspapers. Dr. Bond should have been more specific in his will. One should be prepared to die suddenly. After the hospital was paid for, the widow got everything else, leaving nothing for the son.

"And she's making pridey use of it, let me tell you, mister." The bewhiskered man chauffeured the conversation, taking the verbal reins in his own hands. "She's spending as though she had a bottomless purse! Tripping all over the country in motor cars. Why, she even bought a brand new Whippet—and drives it herself! Money doesn't last forever, but as wealthy as that woman is, it can last a mighty long time—"

"Thank you for the directions, sir." William turned to walk away.

"You're not going to *visit* her, are you?"

"My mother is a distant relative. Yes, we planned to drop by."

"Well, blow me down!" The man took off his seedy hat, put it over his heart and peered toward Martha. "I'm standing here talking to *society*. Should have known by that flossy hat."

Strange sights and sounds pulled at Martha's senses. "Who'd want to live in th' midst o' this raffle an' racket?" she asked, looking from side to side. "I'd go scatty-boo! Sech a soul-disquietin' place! How did my poor Chester abide it?"

The house they sought usurped a whole city block. William parked by the curb and helped Martha from the car. He started to escort her.

"No, you stay right here, William. Stay with th' horse-less. We wouldn't want nobody joyridin' it away whiles we had our backs a-turned. This is a woman-ta-woman talk anyhow. I don't know how long ner short it may take. All yore ta do is wait for me an' take me back home when I decide it's time." She marched up the cobblestone walk-way with her head high and her "hackles up" as Sally would say.

A butler met Martha at the door. The little fellow wasted no words. "Sorry, ma'am. No solicitors."

"No what?"

"Solicitors."

Martha gave him a cold stare. "Whatever that is, I ain't!"

"Your calling card, please."

"My what?"

"Mrs. Bond must know who is calling." It was a long sentence for the short man.

Martha thought fast. "I'll tell her myself, if you please. My son brung me all th' way from Cleburne in his new autymobile ta make this call. I must speak with th' lady."

He disappeared, abandoning Martha to the terrors of the receiving room. She saw herself—and her hat— repeated in an oval mirror on the wall. The reflection was so clear, she jumped. Her hat was crooked, and stray wisps of gray hair stole from beneath the retainer in open rebellion. Some of her courage melted and dripped away. She wished herself back on the farm and would have turned and fled had she not remembered her resolve to help Chester.

On another wall hung the life-sized picture of a blond-haired lass of about seven. That must be Candice. Martha's cheeks flamed red and she wanted to turn her head away so as not to witness the shame of such a scant-ily clad child. Why would anyone photograph a girl in such a short, skimpy skirt? Her arms were flung over her head, and one leg strutted out awkwardly while she stood on tiptoe on the other foot. A dance of some sort? Her lips had been tinted pink, her eyes a duck-egg blue.

Martha felt a world removed from the pomp about her. How could Chester ever have fit here? How could he have been comfortable? *Mayhap he wasn't. Mayhap he endured it only for his wife.*

Hortense sashayed into the room, her perfume hover-ing about her like a bodyguard. Nonplussed, Martha ana-lyzed her in one swoop of a glance. She could have been pretty like her daughter. But the fret lines about her mouth told a story of spoiled dissatisfaction, and the way she held her head revealed her poisonous pride. Selfishness spoke from her charcoal eyes; her dress exposed her desire for attention. Underneath it all, Martha saw an empty, unhappy woman who needed life's greatest gift— and she blinked back tears of pity for this rich lady.

"Yes?" Hortense didn't smile. She looked angry. "You wished to see me?"

"Fer a fact, I did."

Hortense backed up a step, offended.

"I'm Marthy Harris, Chester's mama."

Hortense backed up another step.

"Chester's at home a-grievin' with no paddin' ta lay his grief down on. It ain't fair. I come ta find out how an' when an' why his wife died all of a sudden-like."

"Go away."

"No, I ain't goin' away."

"I insist."

"If you won't answer my questions, I'll ask 'round th' neighbors. Be sure I'll find out fore I leave this town." She narrowed her eyes and pinned Hortense to the wall with her look. *"Cause I don't believe Candice is dead!"*

"Why, Mrs. Harris! Why . . . how . . . how ridiculous!" She made a thin half-laughing, half-crying sound. "Would I *lie* about such a dreadful thing?"

"Would ya? That's what I'm wonderin'."

"If Chester is hurting, can you suppose how much *worse* it is for *me, a mother*? Do you have daughters?"

"Yes."

"What if one of your own daughters should meet with an unfortunate death?"

Martha faltered. Had her intuition been wrong? The

38

whole framework of her suspicions teetered on the edge of collapse. She really had no grounds for the hasty conclusion she made back at Brazos Point.

When Martha didn't answer but only stared, Hortense's voice slipped into a plaintive minor key. "Please believe me, Mrs. Harris. You must!"

Martha held her ground. "Then give me somthin' ta build my balievin' on, Mrs.—"

"Hortense Bond."

"Show me th' death certificate or a pressed flower from th' grave er a deceased date in th' middle of yer fam'ly Bible."

With a hesitation that would have been unnoticed by a person less perceptive than Martha Harris, Hortense's words purred on. "I don't have any evidence yet, Mrs. Harris. But I'll send you a copy of the coroner's notice as soon as it arrives in the mail."

Stalling for time, Martha thought, her intimidation shrinking.

"Candice was an incorrigible young lady as you have probably discerned. I discouraged her marriage to your son because I knew she would never stay with him. Of course, it broke my heart when they parted. Such a lovely young man, your Chester."

Martha let the talk sift through her thoughts. *She can lie easier than I can truth.*

"She had gone to visit my sister in Quebec when that terrible influenza epidemic broke out." Her story unrolled like a runaway ball of yarn. "That plague took twenty million people out of this world! Candice and her boyfriend were among the statistics." She paused. "You'll please not let Chester know that she had a lover?"

Martha said nothing.

"Being so far a distance, I didn't get to go to her funeral myself. The danger of catching the virus was so grave they wouldn't allow me there."

"Ifn it had been one o' mine, I'd'a went whatsomever they allowed."

"My sister laid her away properly, and I'll be forever indebted to her." Her voice seemed milked of emotion.

The haggard form of a young woman hurled down the staircase. "Cook told me you were here!" She screamed at Hortense. "I *demand* that you tell me where—" She saw Martha Harris and folded her tirade in the middle.

"*Can—Can't* you see that I have a guest?" barked Hortense. "Go back to your bedroom at once! I see that you haven't had your tea." The young woman turned and fled as if she had seen a ghost.

Martha couldn't decide whether to listen to her intuition or to ignore it. This hollow-eyed girl bore little resemblance to the Candice that Martha had met only once.

"Who was that?" she demanded.

"My sister's daughter," Hortense said velvetly. "She is Candice's age, and they were as close as twin sisters. My niece became nearly demented when she lost her cousin, so my sister sent her to me. We put sedatives in her tea to keep her manageable. I'm sorry you had to witness such a scene. We go through this every day, but I promised my sister that I wouldn't put her in an institution. The doctor says that with time she will recover from the shock. Everything is so fresh on her mind. . . ." The talk sputtered and died. There was nothing more to be accomplished.

Martha took her leave with a distasteful conviction

thundering loudly within her. *All I've heard today is lies, and I've no way to prove it.*

The butler bowed at the waist as he let her out the door. "G'day, ma'am."

"Ready to go?" William asked.

"Ready ta flee!" A gust of wind grappled at Martha's hat while rounding up the smell of wisteria and the odor of dry box.

"Is your mind at ease now? Will Chester's heart be relieved?"

"I hope so. Candice died in th' epidemic up in th' North. So her maw says, anyhow."

"At least Chester will know."

"But Candice is still alive. I saw her with my own eyes today."

"Mama! Are you feeling well?"

"Never been sounder o' mind, son. An' I ain't losin' it."

"Why would her mother send a telegram telling Chester that Candice is dead if she isn't?"

"She'd go ta any devious devilment to unlock her daughter from our Chester."

"That . . . doesn't make sense."

"To me it does. Them kind er underhandish."

"And you plan to tell Chester that Candice is alive?"

"No. There's a bitsy chance that I could be wrong. Mrs. Bond said th' girl I saw was her niece. But I *know* by my feeler inside that it was Candice. An' her maw *almost* called out her name 'fore she caught herself. Th' girl run like a scared rabbit when she saw me. She recognized me." Martha stopped for breath. "You mustn't tell nary a soul, William. If Hortense Bond doesn't want our Chester bad enough ta lie, no daughter o' hers deserves him! Let him think she's dead so's he can ferget her!"

"It might not be that easy, Mama."

"I'd like ta have a broom big enough to sweep th' pride out o' that woman's gizzard an' leave her a-sneezin'!"

"What if Chester should decide to marry again? It could cause big problems if he thinks Candice dead and she isn't. Having two wives at once is against the law."

Martha frowned at the thought of that complexity. "An' immoral," she said, milling it over. "Howsomever, I don't 'spect Chester will ever want another wife after one like that'n. Ifn he does, we'll jist face that problem when it gets here. Henry always allowed we shouldn't borrow trouble. . . ."

William never knew whether Martha liked his car or whether she didn't.

CHAPTER 5

The Party

Hortense Bond had contemplated the possibility of a confrontation with Chester or his family. She was glad it was over. Candice had almost ruined the whole farce by her abrupt appearance, but it was evident that Martha Harris did not recognize her.

Obtaining a false death certificate would pose no problem for Hortense. Money could conveniently encourage any vice, and with her connection to the hospital, no one would be the worse for the fraud. She had gone this far, and she would not stop until she had completely blotted Chester Harris from her daughter's life. With her husband, Randolph Bond, out of the way, it would be easier. It was Randolph who encouraged Candice to stay with Chester.

If this didn't work, she would try something else. . . .

Hortense was spoiled to getting what she wanted, experiencing no guilt for her actions. That she hastened her husband to an early grave, drove her daughter to emotional prostration, and robbed her son of his rightful inheritance—all for her own selfish passions—gave her no qualms at all. Given the chance, she would have run roughshod over heaven's angels to have her way.

Hortense told herself that Candice harbored a childish rebellion just now, but she would bounce back to her glamorous self when she learned that she could never have Chester back. The past had been unfortunate, but it must be forgotten. This stubborn daughter *would* bend to her wishes. The bridle and reins were Hortense's money. Candice would be lost without the benefit of wealth.

Another party . . . that would help. In her younger days, Candice thrived on parties. Petulance, pouting, or pathos found its panacea in a party.

When Hortense gave the order for the house party, servants skittered like bugs on water to obey her commands. Seamstresses measured Candice for a new ball gown. Invitations, fashioned in fancy calligraphy, went out. Candice's nurse was ordered to withhold the usual sedatives from Candice's tea so that she would be able to dance on steady feet.

Hortense was pleased to find that her daughter fell into the planning with interest. "But I'll need new jewels, Mother," she said. "A necklace, bracelets, earrings. And a tiara for my hair. And please, I don't want anything tasteless. The stones must be genuine, or I simply won't wear them. And may I have a jeweled handbag, too? Perhaps you would let me go with you to choose the diamonds?"

Her mother smiled dotingly. Ah, this was her old Candice back again! The girl had thrown off the brown cocoon and was emerging a splendid butterfly. Here was her "before Chester" darling, wanting expensive clothing and accessories. The wait had been long and tiring, but the wind from these words inflated Hortense's proud spirit.

"Of course, dear. I'll call our best jeweler. I'll give you the money to get exactly what you wish. We won't settle for less." She patted Candice. "This is your 'coming out of bondage' ball, and I'm ever so glad to see that you are cooperating so nicely." She made a prissy mouth. "I hope you won't mind. I have invited a special guest just for you. Remember Chadwich Ross, our banker's son? He's such a dashing gentleman! His mother tells me that he and his wife are estranged and that he is anxious to meet someone *his kind*. You will encourage his attention, of course?"

"Certainly! And thank you, Mother. Are you quite sure he will be here?"

"I will see that he is here and that you have a chance to impress him quite properly."

"Please do."

"You should have married someone like Chadwick instead of that holy-holy chimney sweep from the country who wasted his time and our money in medical training. Give him a threadbare black bag and a mule and he would be in his element!" She gave a coarse laugh.

Candice turned her head and looked out the window.

The Bond mansion buzzed with activity—and with gossip. Rumor had it that Candice was allotted a thousand dollars to spend on jewels.

"The girl is transformed!" the housekeeper said.

"She would have been transformed long ago if the madam would have left off the drugs in her tea." The cook's eyes snapped. "I say it was a shame to keep a young thing like that drugged for so long."

"Why didn't you report it?"

"And lose my job? It would be my word against hers, and who would believe me? Mrs. Bond would say the drugs were ordered by the doctor."

"There's a bad history," whispered the maid. "The madam busted up the girl's marriage and took control of her life through drugs."

"Some gentleman called the other day asking about the miss's *death*. But I remembered Mrs. Bond swearing us to give out no information, so I played dumb."

"It's a joy to see the bit of a thing smile again."

On the Friday night of the party, Candice wore her hair piled in a pyramid of curls, her new jewels winking against the backdrop of the sea blue formal her mother had ordered for her.

When Hortense saw her, she frowned. "A thousand dollars for those pieces, Candice? They look absolutely sleazy to me! I'll have a talk with the jeweler. If they are fake, he will be sued!"

"They're what I wanted, Mother."

"I see that I should have made the choice myself."

"Don't let it ruin your evening."

"If I had time, I'd call the jeweler now—"

"It's much too late. The guests are arriving."

Hortense looked up. "Yes! It's Chadwick. And how handsome he looks tonight!"

Chadwick Ross's grimace could have been mistaken for a smile. He kept pulling at his collar as if it were a noose about his neck. It was obvious that he had been coerced into attending the function by his domineering mother. He paid no mind to Candice until his mother hauled him to her side for a formal introduction. He bowed over the hand he was offered in a half-hearted acknowledgment. Then their eyes met.

What happened neither could have put into words, but misery recognized its counterpart. They were each in deep pain, imprisoned by the social order and looking for an escape. Neither of them could have described the other's physical appearance or clothing. The bonding was a spiritual thing unrelated to earth's passions.

When the music reached a volume to drown out the sound of their voices, Candice whispered the urgent words to Chadwick: "Please help me get away from here."

From there, Chadwick took matters into his own hands. He sought out Hortense and his own mother, who were never far apart.

"It's ever so fortunate that we met on the sea voyage," Mrs. Ross was saying.

"Yes, yes. And now our children have met. It was love at first sight for them. Aren't they a perfect pair?"

"Excuse me." Chadwick touched Hortense's arm. "Your beautiful Candice needs some fresh air. With your permission, I will take her for a little ride in Mother's roadster." It was a double request, requiring the assent of both ladies.

Mrs. Ross winked at Hortense, a conspiratorial gesture. Things were working even better—and faster—than they had hoped.

"Why, how nice of you!" chirped Hortense. "We will beg you both excused. And of course, we will tell the other guests that you will be right back."

"And the car, Mother?"

"Surely, Chadwick. As long as you wish. Take great care of Miss Candice."

Chadwick hurried back to Candice. "You are to come with me," he said as he led her from the Babel of activity in the great house, feeling envious eyes on his back.

Candice knew without asking that Chadwick had a scheme to help her to freedom. She stopped by the hall closet and picked up a pillow slip filled with clothing she had stored there in the middle of the night.

"Where do you wish to go?" he asked.

"To the train station, please."

"Are you . . . running away?"

"Yes."

"I'm afraid I will feel responsible if anything should happen to you."

"I can take care of myself."

"Have you the means to purchase a ticket?"

"Yes. I had planned to sell the jewels my mother bought for me, but she gave me the money to buy for myself. I bought these," she jangled her bracelet, "for less than ten. I knew I would need the money. It's in my handbag." She gave her purse a pat.

He said nothing more until they were in the car. "Pardon me for prying, but is your life at home so unpleasant?"

Candice held her body against a shudder. "Yes! My mother is destroying me! She puts drugs in my tea to keep me from *remembering*. You see, I . . . I have a baby somewhere. And I . . . *I must find her!*" She buried her face in her hands and sobbed.

"And which direction will you be traveling?"

"West. To Arizona. I'm going back to where . . . to where she was born . . . and . . . and never give up my search until she's in my arms!"

Chadwick twisted around in the seat. "You are a brave

lady. If you can do it, then I can, too."

"Oh, no, I wouldn't ask you to help me. It may take months. Or even years."

"No, I mean if you are brave enough to break away, being a lady, then as a man I should have as much backbone."

"I'm afraid I don't understand."

"I, too, have someone . . . a lovely wife many miles from here. My mother sent me a ticket for an emergency trip home. Supposedly, my father was quite ill. When I arrived, I realized it was just a ruse to separate me from Lydia. My mother never approved of my marriage—"

"I . . . I understand."

"But I'm going back to Lydia. I'm miserable without her. Would you mind if I travel along with you?"

"Will you be going . . . the same direction?"

"Lydia is in California."

"I've never traveled alone. I'll feel . . . safer with you along." A high, jittery laugh showed Candice's relief. "But what will we do with your mother's automobile?"

"I'll leave a message with the ticket agent to call Mother to come and pick it up. She'll guess the rest."

CHAPTER 6

Conclusions Awry

Arlene Ross hid a yawn behind her hand. The clock struck midnight as the two plotting mothers sat on the sofa awaiting the return of their children. All the guests had departed in a state of bewilderment. The party had gone flat toward the end. Hortense Bond had lost interest in entertaining them.

"I do hope that my husband doesn't awaken and become alarmed," Arlene said. "However, Roger is a heavy sleeper."

"Do you think you should ring him up?"

"Oh, no. Chadwick and Candice will be back any time now with a wonderful new closeness."

Chadwick and Candice. Hortense tasted the words and liked the taste. "Even their names sound lovely together, don't they?"

"They are a perfect couple in every way," Arlene agreed. "Socially. Financially. Culturally. It is a shame that Candice is still married."

"Oh, but she doesn't know that!" Hortense snorted. "I told her that Chester has taken another wife. And she believes it! I sent Chester Harris a telegram that Candice had passed away—"

"Why, Hortense!"

"The nosy Mama Harris came demanding proof of Candice's death last week. I have a false death certificate in my handbag."

"Such cleverness!"

"I couldn't allow Candice to waste the rest of her life on a no-account, Arlene. You simply can't imagine how mismatched those two were. Chester was raw-boned country, savagely country. *He crumbled his cornbread in his milk!*"

"Chadwick's Lydia wasn't *that* crude. They just didn't have anything in common. She was sanctimoniously religious. She didn't take to dancing, drinking, or the theater—and she had a hang-up about *modesty*. She wanted *everything* covered, chin to toes."

"Ah, ah," tutted Hortense. "There you have it: class difference. It never works."

"I've had a wretched time keeping Chadwick from going back to Lydia. He very nearly talked his father into sending him back this week. It has been a fight up until tonight. Then quite suddenly he was taken with your Candice. Hortense, I can't begin to tell you what a relief it is to know that someone who is worthy of a banker's son has taken his heart! And now to learn that she is not *truly* married . . ."

The clanging of the telephone cut across their chatter. Hortense snatched at it, a look of fright on her face. "Oh, I hope nothing has happened. . . . Hello? Hello. Yes, Mrs.

Ross is here."

She turned to her friend. "It is for you."

"Is it Roger?" mouthed Arlene.

Hortense shook her head, her lips forming a wordless no.

"Hello? Oh, hello? Yes? My car? The train—"

"Oh, no! Oh, no, no, no!" shrieked Hortense. "Our children have been hit by the train! My precious, precious Candice!" She grabbed her chest, went into a swoon, and fainted on the couch.

"Hortense! Hortense!" Arlene called, covering the mouthpiece. "Listen! It's not what you think—" then back into the phone, "I'm sorry for the disturbance, sir. Yes, I'll be there to pick up my roadster in the morning. And thank you."

Arlene hung up and rang for the butler, who appeared on the run, sleepy-eyed and in his nightshirt. "I fear that Mrs. Bond has had a heart failure. Get some smelling salts and quickly!" The man left at a greater speed than he came.

Hortense roused, moaning: "Not my little Candice . . ."

Arlene shook her. "Hortense, listen to me! It's not what you think. Chadwick and Candice have *eloped*. That was the agent at the train station asking me to come and pick up my car in the morning. Our children left on the midnight train *together.*"

Hortense jumped up and hugged Arlene as if nothing had put her into shock. "Oh, Arlene! What a perfect solution for both of us! There's no one in the world I had rather Candice run away with. The banker's son! I couldn't have hoped for a more ideal ending for this evening. Of course, they will be home after their honeymoon. Which direction did they travel?"

"I didn't ask. But I'd wager they went east. Chadwick will want to get as far away from Lydia as possible so that she can't follow him and cause trouble."

"East . . ." Hortense's eyes took on a dreamy glaze. "Ah, yes. The Atlantic. A cruise. Perfect in the springtime . . ."

The servant burst into the room, breathing hard. His hair was askew and his eyes bloodshot. "Here's the—"

"Harkins! How dare you to appear in such an undignified manner! Look at you! If the house was on fire, it would be no excuse for such vulgarity. This is grounds for immediate dismissal!"

"But, ma'am, the lady . . . your guest . . . she—"

"I don't care—"

"I called for smelling salts, Hortense."

"Oh, do you need them, Arlene? You look quite well to me. You should have told me that you were ill—"

"No, Hortense, it was you who—"

"I need nothing at all," Hortense declared with an air of smugness. "I've never felt better in my life!"

The servant fled like a sleepwalker trying to escape a nightmare.

"Such a dunce!" Hortense glared after him.

"All servants are dunces."

"Will Chadwick and Candice's marriage be legal?" continued Hortense as if there had been no break in the discussion of their children.

"We'll get it legalized. What is wrong with a few days of illegal love anyhow? Who will be the worse for it? I say illegal right is better than legal wrong."

"That's what I tried to tell Randolph when he was living, but I could never make him see it my way. No couple could have been more unequally yoked together than Randolph and I."

"I only wish Chadwick would have informed me of his destination so that I might wire him some money."

"Candice had none."

"Chadwick had very little himself. But he will be calling the bank for funds before long, I venture."

"And Candice had no wardrobe save the ball gown she had on. That *will* make a gorgeous wedding dress, though, don't you think?"

"That frothy blue, yes! And as soon as we hear from them, we'll wire enough for whatever they need to have a lovely time. Love may be blind, but we won't let it go *broke!*" Arlene giggled girlishly.

"I've never seen anyone fall in love so quickly. I had never believed in instant love, but I witnessed it tonight. I even *felt* it when their eyes met."

"This is so romantic." Arlene hugged herself. "Roger hasn't a romantic bone in his body. All he thinks of is money, another dollar. He's in love with his position at the bank. But Chadwick was always a loving sort."

"Did you notice Candice's jewels?"

There was a moment's hesitation. "Y-yes."

"Candice paid a thousand dollars for them. How could I have known that those jewels were my wedding gift to my daughter? *I* didn't like them at all, but this modern generation has newfangled ideas. *I* thought they looked cheap, artificial."

"I'll have to concur with you, Hortense. They did look fake. I'd suggest that you change jewelers. But I'm sure if Candice liked them, so will Chadwick. Lydia never wore jewelry, so Chadwick isn't a good judge of quality anyhow."

"Should we call your husband?"

"Heavens, no! Not tonight! He'd be upset for Lydia. Roger rather liked Lydia. But he'll get over it with time, and he'll love Candice as dearly I'm sure. Roger wanted Chadwick to come back here and go into the banking business with him. Chadwick can make good money at the bank. His return will compensate for Roger's disappointment about Lydia. Roger thinks marriage should be an everlasting covenant. He still lives with a nineteenth-century mentality. I keep telling him that we are in the twentieth century now and he should join us."

"You will spend the night?"

"Please allow me to be your guest. I can't retrieve my car until morning. The station agent was closing when he called. Chadwick specifically asked that he call before he left the depot so that we would not be worried."

"Such a thoughtful son! Then let's have some tea, Arlene, and talk awhile. We need to get to know each other's children better now that we will all be family. I don't think I can sleep a wink tonight if I try. I'm much too excited."

"My sentiments exactly."

CHAPTER 7

The Expose

"**Y**ou remember when I took Candice to Scottsdale, don't you, Arlene?" Hortense sipped her tea.

"That was about five years ago? After our Catalina tour?"

"Thereabout. I took her to Arizona to get her away from Chester Harris. When we got back from that tour, I learned that Chester's protracted plans were to become a *children's* doctor. He had all but promised Randolph and me that he would become a famous heart surgeon. I can't tell you how his betrayal angered me! But what upset me even more was that Candice stood by his decision! She was excited about it and was even toying with the idea of becoming his nurse."

"No!"

"Yes."

"Candice, a nurse?"

"It was unthinkable. Granted, I had to give her a few drugs to subdue her, but I knew she would eventually appreciate me for my obdurateness in the matter."

Arlene reached out and touched Hortense's hand. "And we have lived to see that day, haven't we? Today your perseverance paid off. But do go on with your story."

"I left Chester Harris a note—in Candice's name—telling him that the marriage was over and that she never wanted to see him again. Then I arranged for us to have a nice studio apartment in Scottsdale for the winter months so that I could talk some sense into Candice's stubborn little head."

"Why Scottsdale, Hortense?"

"It is a very *elegant* place. A lot of artists and movie producers go there during the cold weather. I wanted Candice to rub shoulders with the best."

"Rational thinking."

"My plans would have worked perfectly except for one thing—"

"And don't keep me in suspense, please." Arlene leaned forward. "What was that one thing?"

"Candice was with child."

"No! And by that dreadful son-in-law."

"I saw no way but to nip the process in the bud. Such an advent would forever tie us to that uncultured Harris clan. It is the last thing I—or she—would want."

"Did . . . did Candice suffer permanent damage from . . . from the—"

"The medication I gave to her didn't work. I can't imagine why. So there was naught for me to do but put her under the care of a noted physician at a private hospital—and go from there."

"Did your husband know?"

"Oh, no!"

"And she bore the child."

"She did."

Arlene waited for Hortense to go on. Each second of curiosity seemed to precipitate, becoming an individual droplet of eternity. Enough of them could drown an impatient listener. But to push or press seemed rude.

"But, Arlene," Hortense lowered her voice to just above a whisper, "the baby was born in *pitiful* shape. No one would have considered adopting it!"

"The drugs?"

"Of course not! It was poor Harris blood! Tainted blood! There was a cripple in their family. Chester told Candice about her. And Chester actually loved the poor creature."

"Was Candice's baby a boy or a girl?"

"A girl. We . . . that is, I didn't name her. Candice insisted on christening her Chessica, but that would make her seem . . . like a whole individual—like a part of the family. I couldn't let that happen."

"The child died?"

"Unfortunately, no, although she is likely dead by now."

"Then what . . . where . . . ?"

"It was a most dreadful experience, Arlene. I've tried to put it out of my mind, but since Candice is to be your daughter-in-law, I suppose you have the right to know. The baby's legs were bent out of shape. The doctor said it would never be able to stand or walk. It would require lifetime care.

"Can you imagine Candice with a daughter who could not learn ballet? Or dance? Can you picture Candice caring for an invalid? I tell you, I couldn't bear the thought! A granddaughter of mine groveling on the ground? A granddaughter of mine who wasn't the belle of the ball? I'd rather have no granddaughter at all than one less than perfect!" Her voice rose a whole octave.

"Did Candice see her child?"

"Absolutely not. The doctor said if I was going to take the baby from her, I must never let her see it, never allow the bonding to begin. He said that the mothering instinct was so strong in Candice that she would give up her health, her leisure even her love for *me*, to keep the child if she saw it once. And, Arlene, the night nurse caught Candice sneaking down the hall in the middle of the night trying to find the infant! I had to have the baby removed and placed in another facility."

"Did your doctor agree with your decision?"

"That one didn't, but I hired one who did. The new doctor conceded that caring for an invalid might not pose a problem for Candice for a few months—or even two or three years. But there were adult years to consider. He said a little hurt now was better than a big hurt later on. Candice would one day feel cheated, he pointed out, when all her friends went on cruises, to balls, or on vacations while she sat at home in a wrinkled bathrobe with her crippled child." Hortense shuddered. "He said I was only showing my love for my daughter by wanting to spare her all this.

"The things he said really made sense. He said Candice would likely have more children in the future. Normal children. With an afflicted child such as this in the home, there would be no time or energy left for the healthy children. And that would be a tragedy."

"He was a wise doctor. But what about the father's rights?"

"I told the doctor that Candice was unmarried."

"You could have told him that her husband had drowned. That would have bode better for Candice's reputation."

"Then Chester's folks might have been contacted and they would have come to claim the cripple!"

"Hortense, I must say that you do think better and further ahead than myself."

"Money will open all doors and close all mouths. Candice's character was not put in jeopardy."

"Go on," Arlene egged. "And Candice recovered?"

Hortense sighed. "It was a bitter fight. With her long face, she could have won the cover girl contest for the Book of Lamentations. She wouldn't quit sniveling. I finally took her to a specialist. He said it wouldn't have mattered if Candice's baby had been the picture of health and perfection and she had it in her arms, she would have gone through this depression. Old midwives call it the "baby blues." In medical terms, it is postpartum distress. It happens to scores of new mothers. He described it as a 'letdown' from the manufacturing process of birth. He said that it might be the fear of a loss of some past commodity: a girlish figure, for instance. He assured me that her sudden melancholy did not stem from the baby being taken away, that it had absolutely nothing to do with her emotional upheaval."

"How long—?"

"Candice didn't quit her moping until I gave up and called Randolph to come. He caught a train and came to us at once. When he arrived, Candice got on his sympathy and I thought I had lost the war—"

"Randolph took Candice's side?"

"As usual. He promised her that he would take the baby for a diagnosis to see if corrective surgery would be possible. He left the next day, and Candice began to improve immediately."

"Ah . . . Now it is all coming together in my mind, Hortense! I can tell you the rest of the story myself. That was the big newspaper story that glorified your husband! Dr. Bond had started back here with the child when he had his massive heart attack and died. I remember the headlines *and* the story. The paper said that Dr. Bond had gone West to fetch a sick baby for treatment and had died with the infant in his arms en route to home. I had no idea it was Candice's child."

"Nor did anyone else, I should hope."

"No. The papers gave no hint as to the child's identity. But they made a hero of your late husband."

"It's a pity he couldn't see his halo."

"What became of the child after that?"

"When I went to claim Randolph's body, the baby was gone. I swore to the reporters that I knew nothing about the child."

"How did Candice react to Dr. Bond's death?"

"She went to pieces and blamed me for losing her baby. She thinks that I know where it is, that I have it hidden somewhere. I don't. She insists I should put out *my* funds to locate the child since I was the one who created all the misery for her. In the first place, I don't wish to ever see the child again. Secondly, I have better things to do with my money."

"I understand your position very well."

"When we got home, Chester was gone. I could have predicted that he would migrate to the country practice he had pined for all along. Candice went into another despondency and insisted on contacting him about what had happened. That's when I told her that he had married someone else in her absence and that he had made it clear she was to stay out of his life. She . . . never got over it."

Arlene touched Hortense's hand again, tenderly. "You poor, poor dear. You have been through the plagues of Egypt. But that was all before tonight, my dear lady! Chadwick will so fill Candice's heart and mind that she will forget the traumatic past and make a new life for herself with him. Oh, Chadwick could charm the spots right off a leopard!"

Hortense wept with relief. "I've spent hundreds of dollars on sedatives to keep Candice from bouts of anxiety over those black yesterdays. I'm so glad it is over! You don't think that Chadwick will bolt when he learns her history?"

"Oh, mercy, no! Chadwick has a heart of putty for anyone with a problem. That's how Lydia snagged him. She was a child of poverty, and he felt sorry for her. Never worry. Even now Candice is in his loving arms, as happy as any bride ever could be."

CHAPTER 8

Chester's Search

In two days, Martha returned from her trip to William's. The air of mystery that she brought back with her unsettled Chester. She was too mum, too preoccupied with unreadable thoughts that held her bleached eyes in custody. She walked about as if some knowledge was sealed away in her soul, but she never mentioned Candice's name. Her premonitions had been correct on so many occasions that Chester began to have second thoughts about Candice's death himself. Could Martha be right?

Chester tried to return to work, tried to normalize his life. But his mind was often distracted and his spirit found no peace, no balm. The past could not be laid to rest as long as it was uncertain. Each day brought a new wave of uncertainty that sabotaged his concentration. As he mixed medications, he found himself checking the ingredients three times, four times. *I'll go to Fort Worth and see what I can learn.* How and when the decision took possession of Chester's mind he could not pinpoint, but it wouldn't go away. He had to rid himself of the haunting unknown once and for all.

He laid his plans. He could go by train one morning and return in the evening. Martha, Sally or Sarah would never know that he was gone unless an emergency brought them to his office. Since Sally came to town on Wednesdays to avoid the weekend traffic, he could go to Fort Worth on Saturday. No one minded a doctor taking a day off now and then; they would merely think he had gone to the city for supplies.

The following Saturday, the train whistled into the Fort Worth station with Chester aboard. The iron monster spit fire and smoke in dragonlike fury as it came to a halt. Chester picked up his hat and moved toward the door. The pleasant day would allow him to walk the distance to Mrs. Bond's home.

Near the depot, a well-dressed lady sat in her shiny roadster, frowning. She looked as though she might have been to a party and seemed so distressed that Chester asked if he might be of some assistance.

"It is this moody automobile," she snapped. "I can't get it to start—"

"Let me check it out for you," Chester offered. "It may be something quite simple."

"Sometimes I wish we had retained the shays," she grumbled. "They were so much less complicated." She was out of the vehicle and at Chester's elbow, talking nonstop. "My son drove this car here to the station last evening and left with his bride-to-be on the midnight express. It was running properly then. I can't think what could have happened to it by sitting overnight. I was just on the verge of calling my husband, but he loathes being bothered, especially by me. He doesn't think a *woman* has any brains in her head. My calling him would substantiate his opinion. I am so glad that you came along, and I do hope that you can coax the contraption to start."

Chester propped the right side of the hood up and looked underneath. "It probably isn't getting fire." He found a loose wire. "Now try it again," he said as he lowered the hood and turned the handle to lock it in place. He stepped onto the running board.

The car gave a lurch that put Chester on top of the car. "Put it out of gear, Ma'am!" he yelled.

"My apologies, young man." She put her head out the window and babbled. "I'm just learning to operate this machine and I forgot about this stick in the middle with the knob. Such fickle things these new inventions are!" The motor quieted to an idle, and the framework settled down to a gentle rocking motion.

The woman delved into her beaded handbag. "I would like to pay you for your assistance, young man."

"Oh, not at all! I wouldn't think of taking a penny. I didn't do anything, really."

"But Roger will insist. He's very proper when it comes to wages. He might even want to hire you for his personal mechanic. You did such an *excellent* job."

"I'm afraid I'm no expert, Ma'am. That isn't my line of work. But as a farm boy, we learned to fix whatever was ailing."

"My name is Ross. Arlene Ross. And such a gentlemanly young man you are. I am quite impressed with you. Do you live near our city?"

"I'm afraid not. I just came in on the morning train."

"And your name, sir?"

"Chester Harris."

"Chester Harris? My best friend knew a Chester Harris once. That is, her daughter was married to one Chester Harris. But I'm sure there's no connection. A coincidence, most certainly."

"Possibly not." He felt like an unfenced yard; there was no place to hide. "I was married to Dr. Bond's stepdaughter, Candice."

Arlene evaluated him with a peculiar look. "Oh, you *don't* say! Then you are the . . . *the* Chester Harris. But I thought . . . I mean . . . but you are so *nice*. So much different than. . . ." Here Arlene Ross became completely flustered.

Chester smiled. If she had heard of him through her "best friend" and if that "best friend" was Hortense Bond, the report wouldn't be complimentary. "Tell me, Mrs. Ross," he said, "is Candice well?"

"Oh, yes! Candice is—" just in time, Arlene caught herself. "*Dead*, Mr. Harris. Surely Mrs. Bond informed you?"

"She did. But there were no details. How did she die, Mrs. Ross? When did she die? It is very important that I have some answers. You see, I loved Candice very much." He tried to keep his voice even, but emotion played havoc with it, thinning it. "I . . . I can't go on not knowing. . . ."

"I really can't . . . I really don't know any details, Mr. Harris." Her face reddened. "Hortense has been quite upset. She didn't give me any . . . any specifics . . . and I didn't probe."

"Did she die here in the city hospital?"

Arlene Ross looked thoroughly confused, caught. "I

would suggest, Mr. Harris, that you talk with Mrs. Bond yourself. She will be glad to give you what information she has, I'm sure. I will be glad to take you to her house in exchange for your kindness in repairing my car."

"I'd be grateful to you." He took the passenger seat and said nothing at all on the journey to the Bond residence. The silence was oppressive; it seemed to embarrass and incriminate Arlene Ross. She steered the car feverishly and came to a jerky stop.

"If you will go with me, please—and return me to the train station when I am finished . . ." Chester, unaccustomed to asking favors, stumbled over his own words. He felt like a coward for not wanting to face Hortense Bond alone. "I will be returning to my home today."

"Certainly."

The walk to the front door seemed a thousand miles to Chester. As he neared, he wished it were even farther. Never had he so dreaded an encounter.

Hortense Bond answered the door herself. "Arlene! Did you leave something? Did you retrieve your car?" She was the picture of good cheer. Then she saw Chester. The chagrin on her face as she looked from Chester to Arlene slowly turned to fear.

"What . . . what is going on, Arlene? Are our ch—, that is . . . is Chadwick all right? Where did you pick up Chester, and what need have you of a doctor?" Her tone was accusing.

"Mr. Harris was at the depot and—my car being stranded—he repaired it for me. He has come seeking information on Candice. I . . . I couldn't help him much, knowing so little about her death—"

"You weren't at the train station last evening, were you,

Chester?" Hortense asked nervously.

"Would it have mattered, Mrs. Bond?"

"He came in *this morning*, Hortense," supplied Arlene, emphasizing the time of his arrival.

"What is it you wish to know, Mr. Harris? I have already given all the details to your mother."

"To . . . my mother?"

"Yes. Last week after you received the telegram, she called on me."

"You surely must be mistaken, Mrs. Bond. My mother doesn't travel. She is seventy-two years old. Someone must have posed as my mother . . . and I can't imagine for what reason."

"I am not mistaken, Chester Harris." Hortense's voice grew brittle, agitated. "And why any of you would let her out of her yard in that abominable black hat, I cannot fathom!"

Beads of sweat lined Chester's top lip. What had Martha done now?

"I . . . I was unaware that she had been here. She . . . she didn't share her findings with me, and again I must admit I don't know why. I am rather in the dark, I'm afraid."

"As I told Martha Harris, Candice died in a general epidemic," clipped Hortense, dry-eyed and statistical. "She was visiting my older sister in Quebec. I didn't get to go to her funeral myself."

"Then may I offer my condolences, Mrs. Bond." He reached for her hand, but she drew it back. "You must know how I am suffering." He looked into her face, but it was stony and rigid. "I loved your daughter very dearly, and she loved me."

"I beg to dispute that claim."

Chester ignored her impropriety. "And if you will tell me where she is laid to rest, I will visit her grave—and place a rose there—wherever I must travel. If you haven't already done so, Mrs. Bond, I would like to have a headstone erected."

Arlene Ross cleared her throat with a tiny cough.

"I, that is, my sister is sending the exact location," Hortense said, shifting her eyes and fidgeting. "And I will take care of the monument. We have taken care of Candice all her life, and we will take care of her in her death, thank you."

"A doctor feels mighty helpless, Mrs. Bond, knowing that the one he loved the dearest departed this life unnecessarily. If I had been informed, if I could have been there, perhaps I could have done something to save her."

"I'm sure there was nothing anybody could have done, and dwelling upon it will not help."

"No, I suppose not." The conversation became stilted, difficult. If Candice was dead, her demise had not affected Hortense in any predictable manner. There was not a single tear. Hortense might have been talking about one of the household servants.

"Your mother had the absurd notion that I was lying about my daughter's death. She was quite rude to me." Hortense's eyes, like marquee lights, mirrored her anger. "So I requested a death certificate to satisfy her." She turned about abruptly and went for the document, her back ramrod straight.

"Here!" She whirled and shoved the paper into his hands. "Now don't bother me anymore! There is your proof!"

He groped out, blinded by tears. Back in the car again,

he sat staring at the certificate. He had dared to hope . . . but this piece of paper ended all hope. Candice was really dead.

"Is something wrong, Mr. Harris?" Arlene Ross asked. "Is the certificate not . . . legal?"

Chester hadn't given that a thought. He scanned the contents with his eyes. The date of death was listed as April 8. He had gotten the telegram on April 7. "I wonder why it was filled out *here* if she died *there?*"

"I can't answer that question, Dr. Harris, but believe me, Candice is *gone. Forever gone.* I can witness to that fact and you can trust me. You must go on with your life without her."

Her words rang true.

CHAPTER 9

Chance Meeting

Candice's body sagged on the gray cot, every joint screaming against its hardness. The heat of feverish blood burned her skin, and her head throbbed. Terrible cramps gripped her about the middle. She had been asleep, but for how long she did not know.

The warm, dry air that blew through the open window brought with it the smell of old leather, dust, and sweaty horses. Her room overlooked a livery stable.

How did she get here? Corraling her thoughts with a tight rein, she tried to remember. Chadwick Ross had stayed with her until she found this place. She had registered under her maiden name, Candice Sharp. They had walked west from the depot where the town thinned from business to residential. Sandwiched between these two worlds, she found a dingy stucco boardinghouse with a flat roof onto which other plastered appendages had been added over the years, disfiguring the whole.

"But you don't want to board here," Chadwick insisted.

"Yes, I do, Mr. Ross. My money may have to stretch for many months, and ten dollars a week is all that I am willing to pay for room and board." Her voice had quavered.

"Are you frightened, Candice?"

"Y-yes," she had admitted. "I've never been alone before."

"You will never be alone," he had comforted. "Remember that, Candice. God is always with you. You can call on Him anytime and He will come to you."

"I . . . I don't know Him very well, but my . . . Chester did."

Chadwick advised her to sew a pocket inside her clothing for the bulk of her money. He left his address in California in case she needed him—and then disappeared.

Now she needed God. She had never felt so ill. Her body pleaded for the accustomed drugs. "God," she prayed, "forgive me! Forgive me for letting my husband down! And don't let me die before I find the kind of faith he had! Oh, God, help me now. I need You. . . ."

Mrs. Borden, the proprietress of the hovel, put her head in at the door. "Oh, you're finally awake, Miss Sharp," she said. "I thought I'd have to call the county mortician. I wouldn't have known who else to call. You listed no references."

"Water . . ." the word was a weak excuse for sound.

"Room service is four bits a day, miss. Special services take extra time, and we're short-staffed here. If I catered to all twenty tenants, I wouldn't get any cooking done. And if I start running errands for free, I'll have everybody playing sick all the time just to get room service."

Candice pointed toward her handbag. At that moment, she would have given her entire purse for a drink of cool water.

Mrs. Borden padded away and returned with the water. It was lukewarm and brackish. When Candice drank it, she was seized by another cramp. She doubled with a groan.

"There's a nurse that rooms here, Miss Sharp. Her name is Greta. She's as good as any doctor I've ever seen. When she finishes her shift, I'll send her to prescribe a tonic if you'd like. She probably wouldn't charge much. She has a pity for poor people like you."

"I don't want any . . . drugs."

"She isn't authorized to give drugs."

"Please send her." Candice's eyes were bright with pain.

All day Candice pitched about on the uncomfortable bed, prayers to Chester's God gracing her parched lips. Her thoughts, swayed by the fever, jumped about like an unpredictable cricket. The past fused into a seamless yardage of night and day laced with small threads of light amid the dark. She called for Chester, for her lost child, for her deceased stepfather.

In a flashback, her mother stood over her with a pill in her hand. She took it and pretended to swallow it, actually dropping it down her collar. She knew it was meant to destroy her unborn child. Later she would hear her mother raving because the pill didn't work.

Once she seemed to be back in the small Scottsdale infirmary in a sizeless gown watching the white-faced clock on the wall that was too busy to stop for pain of body or heart. Then her mother was standing over her again. "It's all over, Candice. You must forget. . . ." Forget what?

"Your baby isn't well. The doctor is moving it to Phoenix."

Candice had pretended to be asleep so that she could hear what her mother said to the nurse. And what she learned made her want to retch! Her mother had separated her from Chester . . . and now she planned to separate her from Chester's baby!

There was an argument between her mother and a nurse just outside her door. "I think you should let your daughter see her infant," the nurse insisted.

"By no means!" Hortense Bond hissed.

"I've seen the comfort even a lifeless baby can bring in a mother's arms. Every mother wants to say good-bye to the child to whom she has given birth. The unknown can haunt for a lifetime, leaving a terrible scar on the heart. I would contend that it is a mother's right to make that decision for herself. Your daughter might wish to see and hold her baby regardless of its condition. If you make the decision for her, someday she will hold it against you."

"The doctor and I are handling this, nurse. It is really none of your business. And furthermore, I am dismissing you from my daughter's case. Your dismissal is effective right now."

Candice relived the fights she'd had with her mother, and her tossing on the springless cot accelerated. "I want to name my baby girl Chessica, and I want her to know that she has a mother who loves her no matter how . . . how messed up she is!" she had argued.

"She wouldn't know, Candice," her mother had insisted. "Newborns haven't the capacity to know anything. The doctor says—"

"I don't care what the doctor says! He has never been a

mother! How can he know what is best? He's a cold, professional *man!*"

"Ah, that's good, Candice," Hortense smiled. "I like to see you get angry. The doctor says that is healthy. There's a process of grief, guilt, anger—then finally acceptance. Today there's anger; tomorrow there will be acceptance."

"I will never accept it! Never! I can't live without my baby!" Candice had screamed. "You have taken her from me and I hate you!"

"But one day you will see the wisdom in my decision, and you will love me for it."

Candice moaned, trying to push away the dreadful memories. She smothered her face in the lumpy pillow and fell into a fitful sleep once more.

When she awoke, the fever was gone and her bedding was soaked with perspiration. She had never felt this weak, this helpless.

The nurse, a sweet, sad-eyed woman of indeterminate age, found Candice crying.

"My poor lamb," she crooned gently. "Don't you cry. We'll have you up and going again just in time."

"In time for what?" whispered Candice.

"Why, for whatever it is you came here for."

"I . . . it's a long story."

The nurse, accustomed to the emotional valleys of her patients, pulled up the frayed chair and stationed herself beside the distraught girl, patting her arm. "Then perhaps we can discuss it and try to decide what is best for you." Her tired smile seemed to exact a great toll. "Let's start at the beginning by telling me who you are and where you are from."

"I'm Candice Har— Sharp. And I live . . . I used to live

in Texas."

"Mrs. Borden tells me you have no family, that you were brought here by a friend."

A tear squeezed from Candice's closed eyes, but she made no reply.

"Life can be bleak without dear ones, can't it? But we always have God."

Candice turned her head away.

"How old are you, Candice?"

"Twenty-six."

"And never married?"

"I am . . . I was married. To the most wonderful man in the world. He loved God and he loved me. My mother . . . came between us."

"And what brought you here? Are you on a search for your husband, perhaps?"

"No, I could find him, but he has remarried now. There's another reason I came. . . ."

"Would you like to talk about it?"

"Have you been a nurse for very long, Mrs. Greta?"

"For about ten years. I've always been a good nurse. In fact, I once nursed in a prestigious private clinic in Scottsdale where the rich and famous people came for treatment. But one day about five years ago, something happened at the clinic that went against my conscience. I lost my job over it. I began to pray, and God showed me that He wanted me somewhere else. Since then, I've nursed on my own . . . the indigent, the terminal, the unfortunate. . . ."

"Would you mind if I asked what happened to change your career?"

"A very wealthy lady brought her daughter there. The

daughter was a young, unwed mother. The baby was born a cripple, and the rich lady refused to pay the expenses for the surgeries and long-term care necessary to make the infant well. I had a run-in with that selfish woman. She refused to even let her daughter *see* the baby she had borne. I disagreed with her rights to do that, and she had me fired."

"Would . . . would you remember the woman's name?"

"I don't recall the name. But I've prayed many prayers for that helpless girl."

"Was the name Bond? Hortense Bond?"

"I . . . why, yes! In fact, it was!"

"That was my mother. I am that girl. I wasn't an unwed mother; I was married to Chester Harris."

The nurse blanched, bit her bottom lip. "Oh, I'm sorry for what I said! I meant no harm. How could I have been so . . . so unprofessional. I . . . I didn't know—Oh, this tongue of mine!"

"I'm glad you told me. I don't know why my mother would put me in a bad light, however. I've never been promiscuous."

"Of course not." The nurse tilted her head. "I suppose that was the only means she had of exercising control over the child."

"She . . . she didn't want the child in the world at all. She . . . she would have ended its life before it began if she could have."

"But why?"

"She . . . hated my husband."

"You said he was a wonderful man."

"He was a prince, but what Mother can't control, she tries to destroy. He didn't fit into her social circle. He

79

broke her puppet strings. His principles as well as his definition of true religion differed from hers. I . . . I was caught in the middle. I can see it all now—but it's too late."

"I hope that I haven't said anything to hurt you."

"No, everything you have said is true, Mrs. Greta. Now you'll understand why I am here: to begin my search for my daughter. I didn't know where else to start. Is the doctor who attended me still at the private hospital?"

"The hospital is no longer in operation. It was turned into a resort for pulmonary patients. I believe the doctor went overseas to escape a lawsuit."

"Then how will I ever—"

"It may be difficult to find her. Your little girl was transferred to a charity hospital in Phoenix when your mother refused to assume her medical bills. I tried to keep up with the baby, but she . . . disappeared."

"My stepfather came for her. He planned to take her home to his own hospital—he was a doctor—but he died of a heart seizure before he got there. If I could learn the name she was listed under, it would be easier to trace her. Until I have that information, I'm afraid I can go no further."

"We'll go to the charity hospital and get the records. I'll help you all I can. You deserve it." Greta gave Candice's hand a squeeze, and a comradely smile replaced the forced one. Her eyes were moist. "But first we must get you well."

"Please don't give me drugs, Mrs. Greta. My mother has kept me sedated for . . . years now."

"We'll give you a good purgative and some warm milk."

"How long will it take?"

"To get the medicine and milk?"

"No, for me to get well."

"You'll likely be under the weather for several days yet. Your body has become dependent on the drugs. It takes a long time to break a cycle like that."

"I'll . . .I'll pay you well."

"I want no pay, Candice. I am doing this service for God. He directed me to you and you to me. He will take care of the pay."

Just before dark, Nurse Greta brought the medicine, the milk, and a small basket of fresh fruit. She straightened Candice's coverlet, fluffed her lumpy pillow, then bent to kiss her good night.

The kiss comforted Candice's wracked heart, and before she fell asleep, she had another talk with Chester's God. She thanked Him for sending Greta, a friend in this "far country." Now she had a confidante, a sympathetic listener, a kind and loving caregiver. Greta might even be an angel.

A shiver of excitement raced down Candice's spine. She had never felt so close to God or so sure that she would find her little Chessica. . . .

But it was another two months before she was able to stand on her feet and walk unaided. And every day she fought a new demon as the craving for the drugs clawed at her soul.

CHAPTER 10

Awkward Moment

"**H**ere, let me help you, Grandmam," Susan said, taking the ironstone plates from Martha. "I'll set the table. My hands need a lesson."

"Ever'body'll be lightin' in here in half th' hour fer supper," Martha nodded. "It's hurryin' time. Molly's always been prompty. An' set one fer Chester, too. He's a-comin."

"I wonder what Rufus and Oscar will look like. It's been five years since I've seen my brothers. They were just ready to start in the first primer then. Can you believe, Grandmam, that I will soon be fourteen? I'm most nigh grown!"

"An' sech a lovely lady Nellie is makin' of you."

"Yes, I've the best mother in the world." Her pretty face took on a study. "It isn't often that a body gets two best mothers in one lifetime."

"I'd say yore goodly God-blessed."

"Do you remember the first time you ever saw me?"

"Ah, yes, lassie! How could ever I ferget? A scareder

thang I've never seen. Yore Gran'ma an' Gran'pa Taylor got theirselves stranded down at th' river with a wheel buggy off. My Alan found all o' you most nigh starved clean to death an' sent up here fer food."

"Grandmam was sick, wasn't she?"

"Yes, an' that baby Billy was a-dyin'. We wuz fortunate that th' Harris reunion was goin' full swing an' our Chester was here to doctor Billy. Elsewise he would've expired. Yore Gran'ma Taylor wouldn't come up fer to let Chester examine her. She knew she had a frettin' ailment that would take her on."

"Grandmam, the reason I was scared was because my mother had died and I couldn't talk. I was afraid I would be whipped for not speaking."

"Nobody would beat a body fer somethin' they couldn't help."

"Oh, yes, Grandmam, it happened lots of times."

"An' you was scared o' *me*?"

"Yes. But when you started telling me about Cousin Tilly and her cat named Scaredy-Cat and her fluffy kittens, I forgot to be scared anymore. You know just how to take the scare right out of a child."

"With th' raisin' of ten children, you learn some thangs."

"I want to act properly when my brothers come. Is it right for me not to show sorrow about Grandma and Grandpa Taylor dying? I was with them for such a short time, they don't seem a *part* of me. Now if it was *you* that died, Grandmam Harris, I'd bawl my eyes out—"

"Don't fret yourself, Susan. You'll ladylike jist fine in front o' Molly's family. Like as not, the Taylors won't even be mentioned. . . ."

The door clapper sounded. Susan turned shy, but Billy bounded to the door in a burst of energy. The girl stared in tongue-tied wonder at her brothers, and they at her. It was she who made the first move. "Rufus!" She held out a slim hand. "You are taller than I! How did this happen? I'm the *oldest!*"

"You can talk! Susan, you can really talk! When did you learn? Who taught you?" His voice was not the voice she remembered.

She laughed. "Dr. Chester Harris is my uncle, and he fixed my tongue."

"It was your tongue all the time?"

"Yes. It was latched down with a string. And Uncle Chester saved Billy's life, too. Billy doesn't look as though he was ever sick, does he?"

"No."

"Uncle Chester is coming to join us this evening, and you'll get to meet him. He's the kindest man in the world and the finest doctor."

"Isn't growing up weird?" Oscar's voice slipped in and out of pitch. "We get used to seeing ourselves in the looking glass, and we're not surprised when we change. But we expect everybody else to stay the same as they were. You're a grown woman, Susan!"

"You're not far from manhood yourself, Oscar," she returned. "Look at those muscles."

Oscar blushed. "Grandpa Taylor said one day I was small and awkward, and the next day I was tall—and still awkward!"

The adults clotted into small groups, leaving sister and brothers to their reunion. Chester came into the midst of the rendezvous and was duly introduced.

"Thank you, Doctor, for giving our sister a vocabulary," Rufus bowed over Chester's hand in exaggerated gallantry. "She hasn't stopped talking since we arrived."

"And for saving our wee dying brother," added Oscar, bowing also. "He hasn't stopped chasing the cat."

Chester grinned. He liked these boys, enjoying the chatter they tossed about like a ball.

After supper, the adults passed the evening on the porch. It was Molly who brought up the subject of Candice.

"Mother left Eli and me a little money, Dr. Harris," Molly said, "and we would like to do something in memory of your wife. We have thought and thought, but we have drawn a blank. Maybe you have a suggestion. Is there some cause she championed, something she especially liked that might give us a clue?"

Out of the corner of his eye, Chester saw Martha suck in her breath and glance toward William. An unspoken message seemed to pass between them. The moment was awkward.

"I . . . well . . . it's kind of you, but . . ."

Martha spoke up. "You don't have to do no hasty decidin', Chester. Eli an' Molly will likely give you time ta thank it over."

"Yes, please think about it, Doctor, and let us know."

When the interminable evening slipped into night, Eli and Molly took their leave. Martha excused herself to an unfinished chore, and Chester was alone with William.

"William," Chester's question took no detour, "did you take Mama to Fort Worth to visit Hortense Bond?"

"Why . . . why," he stuttered, "yes, I did, in fact. She asked me to. I thought she would be afraid of the horseless, but she was a sport. She almost lost her hat a time or two, but—"

"Do you know her reason for wanting to go?"

"She said she needed to get some information for you about Candice's death. How did you know she went?"

"I called on Hortense myself, and she told me that Mama had been there."

"So you know that Mama believes Candice is alive— that she is *certain* she is?"

"She has no grounds for such a supposition."

"She does, Chester."

"What could she know that I don't know?"

"She saw Candice for herself."

"I don't know who she may have seen, but it wasn't Candice. Candice is really dead. I had to go and find out for myself."

"And have you never considered that Candice's mother may have lied to you and that it wouldn't be the first time?"

"It wasn't Candice's mother with whom I talked."

"Even one of the household staff could be bribed—"

"I talked with a very reputable and honest lady, a Mrs. Ross, the banker's wife. She is a family friend, and she knew about Candice's death. We discussed it before I ever visited Hortense. She assured me that Candice is gone. She died in an influenza epidemic."

"I see. Then you will need to convince Mama, Chester. She must face the facts head-on."

"Yes. That's why I brought the death certificate with me this afternoon."

"I wish I knew what to say, brother. I'm glad the uncertainty is . . . ended." William bowed his head in silent grief for Chester.

CHAPTER 11

The Nurse's Formula

"Will I ever get well?" With sunken eyes, Candice searched the nurse's face.

"Of course you will!"

"Why is it taking so long?"

"You are not only healing in body, you are healing in your mind and in your spirit. Every part of you was very sick when you came here. Exhaustion and fatigue had levied an outrageous toll on your sensitive nerves. God sent you to be mended . . . and He is using me as the seamstress."

"Will you teach me about God?" Candice's voice held a plea. "I know so little about Him."

"Have you ever read the Bible?"

"No, ma'am."

"I'll bring you one."

"I would be grateful. And please mark which pages I should read first."

"Reading is good, but salvation is a thing of the heart.

89

Your sins must be taken away, Candice."

"Oh, I want them to be! But I don't know how . . . how. . . ."

"Jesus will forgive them. But before He forgives you, you must be willing to forgive others."

Candice fell into a troubled silence. Then she spoke in a strained sort of way. "You mean my mother?"

"Yes. And anyone else you feel has wronged you. If you don't forgive, bitterness starts to take root beneath the surface of your soul. And if you have mistreated anyone, you will need to make it right."

"Will I have to write my mother and tell her where I am?"

"That I do not know, Candice. You will first forgive her in your heart—and then God will show you what to do next."

"What if she . . . finds me and takes me home?"

"One has to do what is right no matter the consequences, dear. When one does what is just and righteous, the results are God's business. He always works for our best. You must trust Him to do that. He can take what seems to be a great disappointment and turn it into a blessing."

"Forgiving and asking God to forgive me is the first step?"

"Yes."

"Then what?"

"When you are well enough, you will need to be baptized."

"But I don't plan to stay here. I'll just go away and leave the church into which I've been baptized for membership. That would seem pointless, would it not?"

"You have the same mistaken idea about baptism that many people have. Baptism is for the *remission of sins*, not to become a member of a church. I'll mark the verse for you. When you have repented and been baptized in the name of Jesus, your sins are blotted out. It is as if you are starting over with no smudges on your life. Repentance and baptism correspond to the death and burial of Jesus. In confessing and forsaking our sins, we die out to our old human nature. Then we are *buried* with Christ in baptism."

"Then what?"

"Do you know what happened after Jesus died and was buried?"

"He . . . He came alive."

"Exactly! And we receive His resurrection power when we are filled with His Spirit! The old 'us' is gone and God lives through us."

"But what if He . . . He doesn't want me?"

"Oh, but He does! He wants everyone. He isn't willing that any should perish. I'll mark that in the Bible, too."

"Are God and Jesus the same, Greta? To whom should I pray?"

"Jesus was God robed in human form. God is a Spirit, but He came into our world in flesh so that He could save us. That's in John's Gospel. John had a beautiful insight as to who Jesus was. He told us that the Word, which was God, became flesh. When Jesus was born, they called Him Immanuel, which means 'God with us.' "

"Please tell me more." Candice's head doddered.

"Later, child. You need to rest. Think on what I have said, and we'll talk more at another time." She slipped out and closed the door.

But Candice couldn't sleep. If what Greta said was true, it was time to get started making things right. She searched up and down every corridor of her heart. Even though Chester was remarried, she owed an apology to his family. She had acted in a condescending manner the year she accompanied Chester to his family reunion. She had even ridiculed their "homespun" prayers, arguing with Chester that prayers should be read from a book written by someone who could make proper use of the English language. How callow she had been! Her attitude had slapped Martha Harris with scorn. Thinking about it now made her want to put her head under the pillow in shame.

Suddenly, forgiving and being forgiven became more important to her than finding her lost child. Nothing mattered so much as righting her soul.

When Greta returned with the Bible, Candice asked for a pen and paper to write some letters. "I see that you are making progress," the nurse said. "When your soul is well, your body will get better."

"I need to write to my mother . . . and Chester's mother, too. I . . . I hope that she is still living. I did her a great injustice and owe her an apology. The heaviness will never leave my heart until I write to her."

"I'm not sure it would be wise to tell her about her son's baby. That would only make her feel worse."

"Oh, no! I wouldn't want to add to her sorrow."

"Someday, when you have found your child, perhaps you can pay her a visit and let her see her grandchild."

"I just want to tell her how sorry I am that I didn't make a good daughter-in-law. It won't bring Chester back, but I would like for her to know that I have changed and that I love her. The letter will be just between me and her. She won't have to let her son know that she got it. I wouldn't wish to do anything to upset his happy life or disturb his new wife."

"I like what I'm seeing, Candice."

"I'll feel better when the letters are written and mailed . . . especially the one to Martha Harris."

"Yes, you'll feel better."

"It has become more important to me than finding my baby."

"I'm . . . I'm afraid I've made very little headway in the search for your baby. The charity hospital turned the records over to your father and closed the case. They had no further contact with the family after her dismissal and know nothing of her whereabouts. It seems we've hit a dead-end road."

"I'll never quit hoping, Greta, but you have showed me that there are issues of greater value than having my own way. If God has it in His plan, I will find my child."

"You might contact the authorities in the city where your father died and ask where the baby was transferred. They should know."

"I do not know where my stepfather died. I only know that it was somewhere between here and Fort Worth. There are a hundred little towns along the way. Mother would never allow me that information. She took care of all the details herself. I suppose she had the baby put . . . away somewhere. And that's the hardest of all to forgive."

"In reading the Bible, you will find that Jesus Himself had some hard things to forgive, Candice. Remember that you cannot do it by yourself, but you can lean on Him to help you."

That night, Candice wrote her letters by the light of the lamp. She was satisfied with Martha Harris's letter, but her mother's didn't come out right. She wrote it over again, but it still didn't sound proper. After a third try, she knew that she would have to go back to Fort Worth to make her amends in person. Her pen could not do it.

CHAPTER 12

Plotting Mothers

Arlene Ross stood in Hortense's sitting room with a letter from her son, Chadwick, in her hands.

"I can't make sense of this, Hortense," she said. "Chadwick didn't ask for a dime in this letter. He says that he is doing well and is very happy."

"Then I'm sure Candice is happy, too. We must let our children grow up, Arlene. Both of them are past twenty-five and cognizant. They are trying to assert their independence. We did the same when we were their ages. I remember how I loathed my mother's interference! Did Chadwick mention anything about the honeymoon?"

"Not a word. He didn't even say where they took their lodging back East. He was so maddeningly noninformative in the message. But they've been burning up the rails! They are in California now."

"California?" Hortense clapped her hands. "Candice will love it!"

Arlene pulled her blackened brows down. "He did

make mention of Lydia. That worries me. He said she sent her greetings and that she is doing well, too. I can't imagine the *three* of them in the same area. Don't you suppose that Candice would be jealous?"

"Not as long as she has Chadwick's undivided attention. Candice isn't given to mistrust."

"Chadwick's address hasn't . . . changed."

"That rather surprises me. You would think he and Candice would want a new setting to start their lives together. If it's a matter of money . . ."

"We can take care of that, can't we?"

"What did Chadwick have to say about Candice?"

Arlene scanned the letter again. "He didn't mention Candice at all. Now that seems strange!"

"I am disconsolate that Candice didn't at least write a note to me along with his letter . . . or send her regards. That's not like Candice. I can't think that she left that angry with me. And I do hope that Chadwick remembers to give her medication. She gets quite agitated without it."

"Don't you suppose she took some with her?"

"I'm afraid she forgot it."

"Could she purchase some there? Or could you mail it to her?"

"Perhaps." She set her lips in a tight line. "The more I think of it, Arlene, the more I think that you and I should make a trip to California and see what is going on. There is no call for them scrimping by on the furnishings that belonged to Lydia. Suppose Lydia is creating problems for them at this very moment—"

"I tend to agree with you, Hortense. I don't like to be left in the dark, and this letter begs a lot of explaining. I may have to get firm with Lydia. Chadwick is such a softie.

I'll tell her to mind her own business and get lost!"

"Will Roger mind if you go?"

"I'll tell Roger that Chadwick is ill and needs me. He will be glad to have me from underfoot so he can spend his *life* at the bank. He probably won't allow us to take the motor, though."

"Oh, indeed no! I wouldn't consider taking mine *or* yours. There are far too many detours to make the trip by highway."

"We wouldn't want to cross the desert this time of year. It will be hot there already."

"And motors are such temperamental rascals."

"We can insist on a private berth on the railcar."

"I think we should leave as soon as possible. Candice may be needing her medication."

With that whirlwind decision made, the two women flew to traveling preparations. Hortense's servants dropped what they were doing to help her pack.

Their luggage arrived at the depot before they did. "Looks like we have enough people coming to fill an entire passenger car," the porter said.

"Only two women, sir," Hortense's butler said.

"All these cases for two women?"

"Yes, sir."

"Are they moving?"

"Just going for a short visit, sir."

The porter mumbled something about being glad it wasn't a long visit.

On the train and headed westward, Hortense and Arlene were obsessed with little else but themselves and their children.

"Did you ever check on those jewels, Hortense?"

"I did. Our jeweler professes to know nothing about any diamonds. He said Candice didn't purchase them from him."

"Where could she have gotten them?"

"That's the mystery. I have called every diamond shop in town. No one owns up to selling them to her."

"They do pass the buck, don't they?"

"I have concluded that your son sent her the jewelry."

"My son would have had better taste."

"If she didn't buy them, I wonder what she did with the money I gave her—"

"Don't try to solve it, Hortense. You'll have time enough to ask her at journey's end. I only hope that she will forget about the invalid child now that she is settled in with Chadwick."

"Oh, she will! Personally, I think her nagging had become a habit. It had become a power struggle between the two of us—she trying to whittle me for clues and I just as determined not to give her any details. Five years is long enough to recuperate from any emotional trauma. Why, I was over Randolph's death in two months! Candice simply needed a change of scenery. Likely, she will not even mention the child to Chadwick."

"How is it that she never found the child?"

"I saw to it that every crack was chinked. I stole the medical records from Randolph's portmanteau before he left Phoenix with the child. I planned to launder the papers and convince Randolph and the world that the baby did not belong to Candice—that her child had not survived. But fortune was with me, and Randolph died. Without documents, nobody knew who the baby was or where Randolph picked her up. I said that I suspected he brought her up from Mexico. I suggested to the authorities that they put the nameless infant in an institution somewhere."

The porter came through checking tickets.

"I thought Chester Harris a rather nice gentleman, Hortense," Arlene began again. "If I had had a daughter he would be the sort I'd want for a son-in-law."

"That's his way. He makes a good first impression. That's why my Candice fell head over heels for him. But underneath that front, he is a wolf in sheep's clothing. He subtly choked off Candice's life with his priggish notions. I caught it just in time to keep Candice from becoming one of those church-going fanatics."

"I almost forgot that Candice was 'dead' when he asked me about her. I almost told him that she was married to my Chadwick!"

"Arlene!"

"He had some questions about the death certificate you had drawn up."

"What . . . what did he say?"

"He asked why the document was issued *here* when Candice died in Quebec."

"You . . . you convinced him that it was authentic, didn't you?"

"That's what friends are for." She laughed, a cold laugh. "I told him, and quite without lying, that Candice was *gone* from his life forever."

"And he was convinced?"

"He was thoroughly convinced."

"Candice blamed me for the breakup of her marriage. Not that it matters now; everything has changed. But at one time, Candice held me accountable for everything.

Would you believe, she even blamed me for Randolph's death—and I was hundreds of miles away from him when he had his heart seizure?"

"How ridiculous!"

"I don't know what I would have done without that wonderful new Dr. Frisco at our hospital. He said that Candice's behavior was normal. He said she would get it out of her system by and by. He advised me to let her rant. These modern physicians that understand the *mind* are simply fabulous, Arlene. Especially Dr. Frisco. He has been so kind to me since I lost Randolph. He has escorted me to dinners and dances and musicals. But my son, James, cannot abide him."

"Why is that?"

"James says Dr. Frisco is not properly trained to be a doctor. He hasn't passed the medical examination."

"I thought your dispute with James was over Randolph's money."

"I offered to share the inheritance with James if he would let me run the hospital as I wished. I wanted to hire Dr. Frisco as the administrator. He had been so thoughtful throughout the tragedy of Randolph's death. James was against it. He said if I couldn't hire 'licensed and principled' practitioners, he didn't care to be associated with the hospital. I can hear him saying it now! I decided if I kowtowed to James, he would take over. So I hired Dr. Frisco."

"I should think you did the right thing, Hortense."

"James didn't like Dr. Frisco's methods. There was some silly incident that put James's back up. The wife of one of his patients consulted with Dr. Frisco, and he told her she just *thought* she was sick—that it was all in her mind—when indeed she was terminally ill. I told James that anyone could be mistaken and he should overlook Dr. Frisco's error. He couldn't. So I gave him the ultimatum. We would do things my way, or I would cut him out."

"Randolph didn't leave a will?"

"No. Well . . . let's say that if he did, it was never located." She winked.

"So you fired James?"

"James walked out. He said he would be his own man, that he preferred a good reputation to all the money in the world. I thought he would cool down and come crawling back, but so far he hasn't." She sighed. "Candice blamed me for alienating James from the family, too. I tell you, Arlene, I have about had it with Candice! And then—" she folded her hands in a prayer-like gesture of thankfulness, "along came your wonderful Chadwick and made life delightful for everyone! Oh, I can hardly wait to visit our happy children!"

CHAPTER 13

The Letter

The slatted porch swing creaked and groaned. Martha sat darning a pair of cotton stockings when the postman came that Wednesday. "Well, looks like I got somethin'," she said. Since Henry's passing, she had a habit of talking aloud to herself.

She laid aside her work and started toward the mailbox. A decided limp slowed her walk. June had been more muggy than usual this year, worsening her arthritis. "I guess I ain't doin' s' bad fer an ole lady peggin' on seventy-three," she reminded herself (aloud again).

Joseph used to get the mail for her when he was a lad. "Life goes backerds," she contemplated. "When I was young an' could spry down to th' post, I had children to do it fer me. Now when I need som'body to run, I hafta do it myself."

Joseph, Martha's firstborn, had brought the letter from her brother-in-law about Effie. Effie, a spastic, had changed all their lives when she came to live with them.

She had saved Sally from a fire when Sally was a baby. "An' it wuz that bent-winged angel what helped me get saved from fire ever'lastin'," Martha was quick to tell anyone who would listen.

Another generation had come along after Joseph, a new generation that ran down the path with letters for Martha also. They were her grandchildren. Now they, too, were growing up and had lost their fascination with the mail. Matilda, Sarah's youngest, was a young lady nearing her fifteenth birthday. It seemed quite impossible to grasp.

There had been good days and bad, and life's fight had worn Martha down. She felt herself weakening even though her children tried to humor her with their you'll-live-forever prattle. Sometimes she caught herself wishing she could have joined Henry in his long sleep while all her children were still united, before Chester's marriage came apart at the seams. Then she could have gone on with pleasant dreams. As it was, she supposed she would have nightmares until Resurrection morning, when all tears would be wiped away.

Chester had a scar on his heart that was long and deep, and it would never go away. The thoughts of that scar made Martha cry. Chester's eyes looked haunted.

She reached the mailbox and drew out a single letter. It would be for Sally, of course. They got their mail together. Then she saw that her own name graced the envelope in an even, pretty handwriting. It made her glad all over again that Effie had taught her to read. Now who would be writing to Martha Harris?

"Hmmm. Ain't Dessie's pen," she mused. "Ner Amy's. Ner Elise's. Ain't none o' mine. I have all mine learned. But it's a lady-hand."

She hobbled back to the porch faster than she came away, forgetting her rheumatic hip. "We'll see," she said, "who sezs what to Marthy." She tapped the letter away from the edge of the envelope and tore the end in one jagged strip, letting the single page fall out. She pulled her pince-nez from her apron pocket and adjusted the apparatus on the bridge of her nose.

"Dear Mrs. Harris," she read, "I hope that this letter finds you in good health. God has been very gracious to me and is healing me in body and soul."

"Well, well," Martha said to the porch swing, "whomsoever it be, they're a child o' Jesus!"

She read on: "In prayer, I felt that I needed to write to you and offer my apologies for the grief I have caused you and your dear family. I was not a Christian when I married your son."

"Why, all my daughters-in-law wuz Christians . . ." she stopped the swaying of the swing. "Except Candice." She jumped and the letter fell to the floor at her feet. "No!" she said. "It can't be Candice!"

She picked the letter up cautiously as if it were hot. She read on. "I acted in a haughty manner at your family reunion the year that I came with Chester, and the memory of my wrong distresses me sorely. I hope that you can find it in your heart to forgive me. I have also asked God's forgiveness."

The envelope fluttered off the porch and into a rosebush.

"A friend told me that the blood of Jesus will erase all my past so that I may start over. I hope to meet you in heaven, my dear Mrs. Harris." It was signed, "With deepest love and respect, Candice."

"Well, blow Marthy down!" she sputtered, failing to notice that Sally had come through the house and onto the porch looking for her. "Candice ain't dead after all! I knowed it!"

"What are you talking about, Mama?" Sally's look suggested that her mother had taken leave of her senses. "What did you say about Candice?"

"Candice *is* alive, Sally. I have here in my hand a letter direct from her. An' sech a lovely letter! Apologizin' fer bein' snooty at our reunion 'way back when she came with Chester."

"Should . . . should we tell Chester about the letter?"

"I don't see why not! Ifn she's made all those nicely changes, she'll like as not be comin' back ta him an' I'll be lovin' her jist like all th' rest of my sons' wives. Er mayhap he'll even go fetch her. When a body asks fer fergivin' from Marthy, that's what they git. But I 'spect Chester got him a letter, too, don't you? Won't he be tickled? I knowed all th' time that Mrs. Bond was pullin' a shenanigan!"

"I was coming to ask what you need in town. Since I'm going anyhow, shall I take the letter in case he didn't get one?"

"Wouldn't do no harm. Th' sooner we can stop his sorrowin' th' better. He ain't near got over th' shock o' that telegram. An' that Mrs. Bond will pay fer her false-facin'."

"Did she write from Fort Worth? Is there a return address on the envelope?"

Martha looked around. "I don't know where th' backin' went. It was right here. Now it's gone. But I 'spect she's with her mother . . . jist where I seen her!"

Sally went directly to Chester's office with the letter.

106

She waited through two examinations and a splint. The good news she held inside her purse made her fidgety and impatient.

"You have news . . . and it's good!" Chester said when he had finished and turned toward her. "Let me guess. Joseph and Amy are coming?"

"Better than that!" she beamed. She held out the letter. "Mama got this on today's post. It is a letter from Candice."

"From . . . *whom?*"

"Go on and read it for yourself. It's from Candice. Honest."

His face drained of color. Sally noticed that his eyes were more hollow than usual. "It . . . can't be. Someone is trying to play a trick on us, and I don't find it amusing. It is . . . cruel."

"Read the letter, then draw your own conclusions."

Sally sat and waited, watching Chester's expressions. At first, his face was inscrutable. The happiness she expected didn't come all at once, but slowly his face lighted up.

"Yes, it is from Candice. I would know her handwriting anywhere. I've never seen anyone duplicate her h's. They look like little highchairs with the tray on top." He folded the letter with care. "No one can know the weight this letter lifts off my mind. Just to know that she was saved, Sally!" He stopped to brush away the tears. "I couldn't bear to think of her as . . . lost. I know that God let this letter get to Mama just for me, to assure me that everything is all right."

"She didn't write to you?"

"No, but that isn't important. What is important is that

now I *know.*"

"You will go to see her?"

"What do you mean?" He looked puzzled.

"I thought perhaps with these apologies, you would get back together—"

"I'd be happy to, but Candice is dead, Sally."

"But the letter—"

"It was dated June 1 and written almost a year before her death. Why it has taken so many months to reach Mama, I can't explain. Likely, one of the servants found it when they cleaned out her room and, supposing she planned to mail it, did it for her."

"Mama thought—"

"I know what Mama thought. But I know what happened and why. God let this letter be found and sent to Mama to give me some peace of mind. I haven't been able to sleep a single night since I got the telegram in April. The thought that she went to meet a Maker she didn't even know was too awful. . . ."

"Of course you are right, Chester. That makes sense. You have a copy of the death certificate. Mama didn't give a thought of it being a belated letter—"

"Now I can go on with my life, Sally. This letter will change everything for me. Someday I might even think about marrying again if God wills it to be so. I . . . I think I might even sleep tonight knowing that my Candice is safe in the arms of Jesus."

Sally left the letter with Chester, completed her shopping, and returned home.

Just before dark, the constable of The Springs rode out to Martha's. "One of Dr. Harris' patients found him passed out in his office," he said. "You'd better send someone for him."

While Sally's husband hitched up the wagon, Martha threw off her apron and dug in the cedar chest for her black pan hat. "When a child o' mine is troublin', I trouble double," she said to the empty room. "We'll go an' bring my boy home, an' I'll git him back strong again. Ever'thang has been too stressy for my Chester these last few weeks. Losin' a mate is life's hardest blow next to losin' a child."

She ran for the wagon as fast as her sciatica would allow.

CHAPTER 14

Alan's Proposal

In his delirium, Chester kept calling for Alan.

"It's like when they wuz wee laddies," Martha said, "always wantin' each other when they wuz in trouble er pained. I guess that's what bein' a twin is all about." She padded out, and when she came back, she told Sally, "I called Alan on th' horn an' he promised to book a passin' on th' next train headin' our direction."

Sally kept spooning Martha's warm broths down Chester's throat, bathing his head with wet washcloths. "When I helped him with Nellie's baby, he said if he was ever ill, he wanted me for his nurse," she said. "Now he's getting his wish."

All of them hoped that Alan's arrival would rouse Chester. But it didn't. He ceased calling for Alan and began calling for Candice.

"That's not a good sign, is it, Alan?" worried Martha.

"He'll be all right, Mama," Alan insisted. "He is overworked."

Martha told Alan about the letter she got from Candice. "It gave me a strike in th' heart like lightnin' when I got it," she said. "But Chester figgered out that it was writ last year an' jist got mailed out recent-like by some of th' servants. We thought th' letter would boost him up, not take him down."

"What did the letter say, Mama?"

"It was a sweet, apologizin' thang that told how she'd made her heart right with the Maker afore she went to meet Him. She told me she'd meet me in heaven."

"Then I can guess what happened. Chester had worried so long over his wife's eternal destination that when he finally got a release from that pressure, he broke. A 'let-up syndrome.' It happens like that many times. Most recover. I think Chester will rally in time. His emotional system needed the rest."

Sally came with another cold compress. "Why didn't you bring Elise, Alan?"

"She was interviewing for a new job, Sally. It's a government experiment that Mr. Jorgensen and I implemented, and Elise is very excited about it. It is a special education program—a pilot program, so to speak—for children at the state home. Each teacher will have no more than five handicapped children to tutor in one day. Representative Jorgensen and I are of the opinion that some of these children are quite brilliant, and we believe they have talents they can contribute to our society. Elise will be teaching the beginners: that would be first grade in the public school system. You know my passion for education and fairness for all.

"Elise won't be starting until September, but she has met the children already and is most optimistic about those who have been assigned to her. She will have two boys and three girls."

"That's what makes your work at the Capitol so special, isn't it, Alan? You are forever trying to find ways to help people who might not be able to get help by any other means."

"It is a rewarding job, Sally. One that I ask God to help me with every day."

In three days' time, Chester was rational again, able to sit on the edge of the bed. He didn't seem surprised to find Alan there.

"I've been through a dark valley, Alan."

"The sun will shine again."

"Yes. I . . . I didn't realize how much I loved Candice . . . and how much blame I took for her soul's poverty when the load wasn't mine to carry at all. I should have trusted God to save her years ago! But it seemed so . . . impossible." He managed a weak smile. "How we limit God, brother! If he could save Saul of Tarsus, he can save anybody!"

"Yes, God can turn a hopeless end into an endless hope."

"I like that."

"When the fight was over, you caved in."

"It was exhaustion, Alan. Physical, mental, and spiritual."

"You need a time of restoration, Chester. You are not going back to work next week. I insist."

"No. I'm a doctor and I know that I need a sabbatical."

"Diagnosis correct! I plan to take you home with me. You need a change of pace, new surroundings for a while. You will love our little storefront church and the friendly people there."

"Thanks for the offer, Alan, but I can't do it."

"Why?"

"You would be at work every day. I'd be home with your wife. You might not mind, and I might not mind. But the neighbors might have something to say about it."

"Not so fast, brother. You should know me well enough to know that I won't jeopardize your character. There's no problem there. Elise will be in training for her new job that starts in September. Then she will be teaching at the state school. In the daytime, you will have the house to yourself—to read, work puzzles, and sleep."

"Does Elise know about it?"

"She will be delighted."

"How will we handle Mama? She fusses over me like a sick calf."

But Martha Harris was quick to agree that it would probably be the best thing for Chester. "Henry always allowed that a new dishrag would perk any kitchen up. That wuz his way o' sayin' changes is good fer a fellow sometime. Now me myself, I wouldn't like th' city bustle an' bangin', but Chester has been there an' can take it on th' ear. Prob'ly he needs somethin' to chase th' quiet away for a few days."

Alan went into town to put a notice on Chester's clinic, informing his clients that the doctor was taking a leave of absence.

"An' we're right gladsome, sonny," an old-timer spat through a gap between brown snags of teeth. "We was eversome worried about him since he got news of that tragedy. He's got this whole community spoiled. Ever' snotty nose runs to him when nature would take care of most. Them mothers can go back to their coal oil and

114

compounds of blackstrop molasses for a few weeks. It'll do them good. You send my word to Dr. Harris to stay recuperating as long as he needs, then add a month for good measure. Tell him Old Man Jacobs what used to run the drugstore said so." He poked his cane at a crack in the paving.

"I'll tell him."

The strain lines began to dissipate from Chester's face when they boarded the train for Austin. Martha, Sally, and Jay stood on the platform waving good-bye.

"Precious mother!" Chester said. "We won't have her forever, Alan. Of late, I've considered that her mind may be already slipping. She finagled William into taking her to Fort Worth after I got the telegram. She came back declaring steadfastly that she had seen Candice. Sometimes I wonder if she has it all straight in her thinking yet!"

"She needs time to forget, and so do you, Chester. When one of her children hurts, it is hard for her to handle."

"I guess that's what makes us love her so."

"I want you to try to forget the past. You've been alone for too long. You need some social life . . . and no one can fix you up with a lady friend better than my Elise!"

Chester turned toward the window, watching the landscape roll and loop into little knots of hills. Alan's last statement made him uncomfortable. The very thought of another woman troubled his spirit. But why? Certainly, he had every right to transplant his heart and start a new life. . . .

He lapsed into his own world of thought, and Alan left him there.

CHAPTER 15

The Discovery

Candice tried to shake her nervousness, but it clung like a burr. She paid no attention to the little river that nibbled its way through the canyon outside the coach's window.

Returning to Fort Worth to make peace with her mother was the hardest decision she had ever been called upon, by God or man, to make. That her mother would again try to take possession of her life she had no doubts. She didn't know how she would manage, but she had made up her mind on one score: she would take no more of the drugs Hortense administered.

Leaving Greta had been hard, too, like a boxcar breaking away from its engine. The Bible in which she had found her answers belonged to Greta, and leaving it behind was like parting with a dear and trusted friend. There were other Bibles, of course, but none marked in the places Greta had highlighted.

Greta had insisted that Candice wasn't strong enough

to travel, but Candice felt an urgency to go. "Then I will pray for you," the nurse said, no longer trying to detain her.

Every town through which the train threaded its way brought the same tormenting question to Candice's mind. Was this the town where Randolph Bond died and left her unidentified baby? She found herself wishing there were no more towns to expose the ragged scar tattooed on her heart.

Relief and dread sat side by side on the bench of her emotions as the locomotive neared her home town. Her palms were sweaty and her feet cold.

She disembarked at the Fort Worth station and looked around. Was it only three months ago that she had left this place with Chadwick Ross? It seemed more like three years.

Chadwick. She had not thought of him, nor had she heard from him since they parted, but she hoped that he was happily reunited with his wife. It seemed a shame that one's own parents would work against what was good and right, but without Christ they sometimes did.

Candice knew that she would never marry again, no matter how much her mother insisted. She had never loved anyone before Chester Harris or since. *And somewhere his child needs me.* The unbidden thought brought a rain of fresh tears.

A derby-capped cab driver sat waiting, hoping for business from the incoming passengers. Candice gathered her grip and hastened toward his conveyance. When she gave her address, the cabby raised his brows. "The rich lady's house, eh?"

If Candice admitted to being "the rich lady's daughter," the driver would expect an enormous fee. She kept quiet.

"If you're going to apply for work there, miss, I'd better

118

warn you that she's mighty hard to work for. Wages aren't in keeping with the palace, either."

"I . . . I'm going there on business."

"She won't lend you any money. She's tight as a new shoe. She even cut her own son out of his inheritance when her husband died. And if she did make you a loan, she would lace you up to your neck about paying it back."

"It isn't money that I'm after, sir."

"Well, luck be with you, miss. You have my sympathy but not my envy."

She paid him a workingman's fare and got out, relieved to be away from his contempt. Her legs trembled, threatening to betray her and leave her body stranded on the manicured lawn.

The butler came to the door. "Welcome home, Miss Candice." He bowed.

"Is Mother home?"

"No'm. She left a week ago today for California to visit you."

"California? To visit me? Who told her that I was in California?"

"Your new husband wrote and—"

"Harkins! What are you talking about? I have no new husband!"

"Why, Miss Candice, you and Mr. Ross left from that party an elopement. I heard your mother and Mrs. Ross gloating over it. They were both pleased as punch. They allowed that you went *east*, though, to get away from Mr. Ross's first wife—"

Candice looked exasperated. "There you go prevaricating again, Harkins. How many times has Mother told you—"

"No'm. I'm truthing, Miss Candice. I heard it with these two good clear ears. Mrs. Bond told everybody that you had gone away and married the banker's son. She was waiting to hear where you honeymooned so she could put it in the society column."

"Well, I didn't! I had no such plans when I left Mother's party. And neither did Mr. Ross. He was returning to his wife and I . . . I had other plans."

"Mrs. Bond surely thought you were in California with Mr. Ross. She and Mr. Ross's mother have gone there; I loaded their luggage myself. They planned to stay for a spell and visit you. But do come on in. Cook will be glad to see you. You can order us around until Mrs. Bond gets back. We're getting spoiled with so much free time and no scolding. I'm afraid Cook is getting lazy. We've had hash for three days in a row."

"Perhaps when Mother finds that I am not in California she will come right on back."

"I'm satisfied that she will."

"Did anyone call for me while I was away?"

"Mr. Harris came."

"He *did*?" Candice's eyes blazed, then the light evaporated when she remembered that he belonged to another woman now. The memory turned vicious and bit deep into her soul. "Why was he here?"

"He came for some sort of document from Mrs. Bond."

"Something to do with the hospital probably."

"I never did know just what. May I carry your bag up to your room?"

"It isn't heavy."

"You aren't akin to your mother when it comes to baggage."

Without her mother's presence, the household seemed jovial, carefree. Candice found herself at ease with the servants, endearing herself to all of them.

"Miss Candice is a plumb different person, isn't she?" the cook mentioned to Harkins. "Something about her has changed. I dread for Mrs. Bond to come back and start filling her with those dreadful drugs again. Those medicines alter Miss Candice's personality."

When Sunday came, Candice asked Harkins to take her to church. When he started toward Hortense's cathedral, Candice objected. "No, Harkins, I don't want a dry, formal church. Do you know where there's a small chapel of common people who really love God?"

"Where they do hallelujahs? Loud?"

"Yes, that kind."

"I can take you to one, Miss Candice, but your mother will be angry with me. I wouldn't want to get myself fired."

"My mother isn't here, Harkins, and she won't know where I go. I'm twenty-six and responsible for my own soul."

"I wish you had thought of that five years ago, miss."

"I do, too. I would still have Chester."

When Candice got home from church, she asked Cook if there was a Bible anywhere about the place.

"There's the Bond family Bible, Miss Candice. Mr. Bond used to read it now and then, but Mrs. Bond never does. It is locked in the library, but I have the key."

"Please get it for me."

Candice took the Bible to her room. She had learned where to find the Gospel of John and had read the Book of Acts several times. She remembered finding the plan of

121

salvation in the second chapter. She especially enjoyed Acts. It was full of miracles.

She was thumbing through the Bible when she saw the newspaper clipping. It was folded between the Old and New Testaments, and a sixth sense urged her to look at it.

Her heart beat fast, then faster. The news item gave the details of Randolph Bond's death. He had an indigent infant in his arms when he passed from this life in Amarillo, the report said. The infant was nameless; no papers could be located on Dr. Bond's person. His wife said that he was en route to home from a trip to Mexico. She supposed he was bringing a patient for treatment. He had a penchant for charity cases, especially children. The baby was turned over to the authorities of Potter County for placement.

Amarillo. Here she had a clue! She must go to Amarillo at once! She rang for Harkins. "I'll be leaving again tomorrow, Harkins. I find that I must go to Amarillo. I have urgent business there."

Harkins frowned. "You look washed up, miss. I think you should rest up a few days and speak with your mother before you go gallivanting off again."

"I will be fine. I really must go."

"Have you plenty of money?"

"I . . . think I have enough."

"Is there an address where your mother can reach you?"

"No, but I shall leave her a note."

"I guess you are old enough to take care of yourself, but you've been dependent for so many years that I can't help but stew."

Early the next morning, Candice was back on the train

and headed for Amarillo. "I will find you, my precious Chessica!" she whispered. "And when I do, we will make up for all the time we have lost!"

She shivered . . . and couldn't tell if it was from joy or the fever that she felt rising in her body.

CHAPTER 16

New Admirer

Helen Jorgensen dabbed on a new smear of lip paint. She hadn't seen her friend, Claire, in two years, and she wanted to appear as chic now as she did then.

They met in the downtown cafe wedged between the law office and the clothier. The eatery had been updated from its chalked-in specials on a slate. Now there were printed menus on every table. The place had changed owners and taken on a more sophisticated air, but Helen noticed that business had slacked off.

Claire came rushing in, bejeweled and overdressed. "Helen! How good to see you and how *marvelous* you look! Now do sit down and condense the last two years of your life into our one short hour together! I'm perishing to know where your zodiac has taken you!"

"It won't be hard to do, Claire. I missed my constellation, and I've been stuck in a rut with that miserable David Briar. Why I didn't file for a divorce sooner, I can't explain to you or to myself. What an abysmal existence!"

125

"I warned you about marrying on the rebound. The wages of not listening to me are my never-ending I-told-you-so's."

"I know, Claire. I should have listened to you. But I was so much in love with Alan Harris and so crushed and lonely when he married that stodgy schoolteacher from the country that I couldn't think rationally. I couldn't bear seeing Alan every day in Father's office, knowing what I had missed.

"Then David came along with his big promises and talk of wealth. But he turned out to be a devil of a drinker and refused to give me a free hand with the bank account. What good is money if you can't *spend* it?"

"Then he created such a *scene* when I went to the theater with one of my old suitors! That was the last straw. When a woman can't even have friends—"

"Helen, you haven't changed at all!"

"I hoped that you would notice."

"And you will be in town awhile?"

She gave a long, tired sigh. "Not unless something interesting develops at once. I can't stay here and *rot.*"

"Something interesting has developed."

"If it concerns any of the dense men around here, forget it. I'm through with them."

"Don't cut your nose off to spite your face, Helen. You've a habit of that. I have one you might want to hear about."

"Not unless it is Alan Harris. I'm not over him yet. I don't know if I will *ever* get over him. His marriage hasn't taken a nose dive, has it?"

"No, it's not Alan—"

"Then spare me."

"It's his twin brother, Chester. Remember the doctor? He is here in Austin now. I've seen him around town with Alan several times."

"The one who is married to your cousin in Fort Worth?"

"*Was* married."

Helen sat at attention, her eyes ignited with a calculating fire. "He's . . . *available?*"

"He is. I took it upon myself to do some sleuthing for you."

"Don't keep me waiting, you miserable tantalizer! Is he as handsome as Alan?"

"They are twins, remember."

"Identical?"

"Close enough."

"Does he have a medical practice here? I can surely come up with some ailment."

"I don't know where he works. He hasn't been here long. He is rooming with Alan."

"What . . . what happened to . . . what was his wife's name?"

"Candice. I asked Mumsy and she said she'd had a letter from Aunt Hortense a couple of months back and that Candice had remarried. She married the banker's son, an old flame of hers. You remember that Uncle Randolph died—"

"Bringing a patient back from Mexico. I read it in the news."

"Aunt Hortense said that Candice and Chester were never compatible."

"I can't imagine being incompatible with a man who is anything like Alan—"

127

"Shhh! Here he comes. . . !"

Chester took a booth, absorbing himself in the study of the menu.

Helen rolled her eyes and fluttered her hand over her heart while Chester's head was down. Claire suppressed a giggle.

When Helen's food came, she didn't touch it. She folded and unfolded her napkin in an anticipatory study. Frequent glances at Chester replaced the outright stare she squelched. "It is as if time has turned back for me," she whispered. "I was enamored with the wrong one all the time. I have just laid eyes on the man for me!"

"You've told me that a dozen times about a dozen different men."

"This is the real thing, Claire. All the others were infatuation."

Before Claire could stop her, Helen slid from her seat onto the bench opposite Chester. No grass grew under her feet when it came to flirtations with men. Claire found herself abandoned with both her lunch and Helen's.

"I'm Helen Jorgensen," she said to Chester, making her eyes wide and innocent. "My friend tells me that you are Alan Harris's brother. State Representative Jorgensen is my father and your brother works with him."

"It is a pleasure to meet you, I'm sure, Miss Jorgensen." Chester smiled. "I don't believe I've heard Alan mention the fact that Mr. Jorgensen had such a lovely daughter."

"I've been away. To school."

"I see. And what is your major?"

"Uh. I . . . plan to teach."

"Alan's wife is a teacher."

"My friend, Claire, is a relative of . . . of the late Dr.

Randolph Bond."

"He was my mentor."

"Claire told me about . . . about . . . your ex-wife—" The pain in Chester's eyes stopped her.

"Yes, it was hard for me to accept. I've come to Austin to . . . to start over, so to speak."

"And what better place, Mr. Harris? I believe it is *Dr.* Harris, is it not?" She favored him with her most practiced artificial smile.

"Just call me Chester, if you wish."

"Oh, I'd be delighted! We all have pasts that we would like to forget, don't we? But I say why pull yesterday's clouds over today's sunshine?" She gave him another cheesy smile.

Chester's own smile was feeble. "It . . . it takes awhile."

"Yes, and one needs diversion. Now that I am home, I will be having some socials," she said. "I'll be throwing some 'let's forget' parties. I will see that you are included, Chester."

"Thank you." Before Helen could regroup her words for another lure, Chester excused himself to an appointment and was gone.

"Now I'm glad I didn't marry Alan Harris, Claire," Helen said, straining to get a last glimpse of Chester's jacket. "Chester is much more refined. Did you hear that mellow voice? I have just had my first conversation with the man with whom I am destined to spend the rest of my life! Oh, isn't this glorious? And won't David Briar gnash his teeth?"

"Mr. Right at last?"

"I am smitten."

That evening, Chester mentioned the meeting to Alan.

"I met your boss's daughter today, Alan."

Alen jerked his head up. "Helen?"

"The same. She is a friendly sort, isn't she? She is bent on including me in the city's social swing."

Alan looked so troubled that Chester laughed. "I can see that you're worried about me, but you can spare yourself. I can't make a *second* mistake. I have my guard up."

"Sometimes those shrewd ladies have a way of taking your heart unawares," Alan warned. "You're vulnerable right now, Chester, and I can't help but be concerned—"

"Don't fret, brother. I've been reading in God's Word about affections. I broke all the rules when I set my affections on Candice." He shook his head. "No. The next woman I choose will be someone quite different from Candice, someone with whom I can worship God. I want a godly home. Your boss's daughter may be lovely, but she is not the woman for me."

CHAPTER 17

Cold Trail

By the time the train reached Amarillo, Candice had a raging fever and a desperate thirst. Her head felt like a gravel-filled bucket, too heavy for the rest of her body. She tried to lift it from its position against the back of the seat and stand to her feet.

She reached the station platform, but as she squeezed her way through the crowd, sound and sight blurred into the distance, small and far away. She felt herself drifting. She thought that her feet were moving, but instead they stood rooted while her body crumpled down about them. Then all was black.

When she awoke, she was in a small room on a bed just wide enough for her frame. The familiar smell told her that she was in a hospital. A crucifix hung on the wall.

"I don't know what it is about these trains, Doctor," she heard a woman's voice saying outside her door, "but this is the second victim since I've worked here. When I first came, they brought in an unconscious man—and he never woke up."

"You're talking about the doctor?"

"Yes. The one with the crippled baby. And now we've had another one brought in from the train station with a dreadfully high fever."

"Nurse . . ." Candice called.

"It sounds as if she is coming to, Doctor." The nurse rushed into the room.

"The doctor . . ." Candice pushed the words out through thick lips, "the one that died. I heard what you said. . . ."

"Now, now. Just because the doctor died doesn't mean that you will die, too, dear. He was an elderly gentleman." She patted Candice like she would a fearful child. "Now don't you fret over what happened to that doctor."

"But . . . but he was my father. Dr. Bond."

"You don't say? What a coincidence! Yes, I recall now that his name was Bond, although I can't remember the first name. It was an unusual name."

"Randolph."

"Yes, Randolph. Almost like Rudolph. One of Santa's reindeer, yes."

"The baby . . . what happened to the baby?"

"It was a girl child. They couldn't find any papers, any name—"

"I know the baby's mother and I . . . I want to find the baby for . . . for her. She's been looking for her."

"The authorities might be able to help you. The sheriff or one of the officers."

"When can I get out of here to talk with them?"

"Oh, mercy! You can't get up for several days, dear. You've been very ill."

"But I must."

"I know Sheriff Simmons, and I'll send him to speak with you if it will make you feel better."

"Oh, please!"

Candice slept little that night, strung up by the brittle thread of hope. She wove a whole future of happiness from the small bit of fabric she gleaned from the nurse. The officer would be able to take her to her little Chessica. Her search would end here in Amarillo.

Sheriff Simmons came. He was a stocky man with a mane of graying hair. "Nurse Jiles tells me that you are looking for the child your father was transferring to his hospital."

"Yes. Her mother is . . . is looking for her."

"I'm sorry that I can't tell you where the infant was placed. The child was healthy except for her crippled feet. We had an elderly lady working for us at that time who offered to place her for us. She has since moved away."

"Where?"

"I don't know her present whereabouts."

"How will I ever find the baby if I don't know her name or where they took her?"

She began to weep.

"Don't cry now. I can give you some information that might help. Since we didn't have a name, we called her Baby Bond for the doctor. The lady who took her planned to place her in a private orphanage in Abilene called The Lamb's Fold. If they were full and couldn't take her, she said she would try to get her in a state facility. The state home is in Austin. We didn't know if there might be a minimum age there, but she planned to check it out. She was a trustworthy woman, and we left the placement up to her. I wish you luck in finding her for the mother." With that, Mr. Simmons left.

He stopped by the nurse's desk. "That's the mother," he cocked his head toward Candice's room. "I'd put my best horse on it."

Determination drove Candice. She choked down un-appetizing food, endured the strenuous exercise, and was appalled at the frightening amount of funds it took to free herself from the hospital. She couldn't afford to be sick again.

The day she was released, she reboarded the train for Abilene, following the tips given by the sheriff. After many inquiries, she found that the orphanage had gone out of business, sending the "lambs" that remained to various charitable institutions. Some were adopted out. No one knew if there had been a Baby Bond registered; five years ago; no one knew where the records of the defunct home went.

Candice had never felt so alone, so defeated. Life for her seemed to be all road and no arriving. She rented herself a cheap room for the night and cried herself to sleep. But as day broke, she awoke with a verse from Greta's Bible flooding through her mind: "Fear thou not; for I am with thee: be not dismayed; for I am thy God: I will strengthen: yea, I will help thee."

She sat in the bare room, trying to decide what to do. She only had enough money left to buy one ticket. Should she go on to Austin or take the train back to Fort Worth?

She knelt and asked God to show her what to do. She heard a voice, so clear that she looked about to see who spoke: *Seek, and ye shall find.* No one was in the room.

She bought a ticket to Austin.

CHAPTER 18

Elise's Pupil

Elise came home each night telling Alan and Chester about "her children" at the state school. She was testing them to determine their intelligence level so that she would know where to start their education. "You can't believe how smart some of these pupils are, Alan!" she bubbled.

Alan loved seeing his wife happy; he thrilled to her enthusiasm. All children responded to her, but that did not surprise him. She was part child herself. She had great faith in Alan's program for the underprivileged children and often told him so. The contagion reached Chester. *What must it be like to live in such a state of harmony with one's companion?* he asked himself.

One day, however, Elise came home pensive and thoughtful. "Is something troubling you, my beautiful?" Alan probed.

"I don't think some of those children are getting the medical attention they need, Alan."

"We'll have to change that, won't we?" He kissed her on the cheek.

"I hope so. The child I was testing today has a chronic cough and a low-grade fever most of the time. She's such a lovely child and so uncomplaining. She reminds me of a pressed flower from . . . another world. She has the most comprehensive eyes! Why, she cheers *me* up when I go into her room! But I don't like the sound of that cough."

"Talk to Chester about it. She probably needs some sunshine."

"They all need sunshine . . . in more ways than one. Some of them never have visitors, Alan! Can you imagine a child with no one to care? That little girl hasn't had a visitor since she has been in the school—and she must be six years old!"

"Uh oh. Those children are stealing your heart!" He slipped his arm around her. "Save some affection for me."

When she laughed, her eyes twinkled. "Who's spoiled?" she teased.

"No one around here!"

"Where is your brother?" she asked.

"He's helping the parson at the church. I thought it would do him good."

"I have someone I want him to meet. She's a new nurse at the school and such a wonderful Christian! She promised to be at church this weekend."

"Good! Chester says I'm not to worry about Helen Jorgensen, but she's dogging his tracks."

"She dogged yours."

"But I had eyes only for you."

Chester came in humming a hymn, shavings of sawdust in his hair. "We built some new benches, Alan," he said. "And when God gets them all filled, we'll build a bigger church."

After supper, Elise asked Chester's opinion on the frail child. "What would cause such an ongoing cough and fever?" she plied.

"Has she been checked for tuberculosis?"

"I don't know. I wish you would come and take a look at her."

"Would the administrator mind?"

"He'd be grateful, Chester. There aren't enough doctors to go around. Each child only gets checked at infrequent intervals or when they are very ill."

"You know, at one time it was my ambition to become a pediatrician. That's the new name for doctors who confine their practice to children. One might add a few years to an older person's life, but when you cure a child, that child has a whole life ahead of him."

"You'll be impressed with this little girl, Chester. Her name is Charity. She has a most fascinating history. I am required to study the background of my students, and this one has an interesting file. Nobody really knows who she is or where she came from. She has never had a visitor in the six or so years that she has been resident at the state school. She was brought in from Amarillo after being pried from a dead doctor's arms. He died of a heart attack on a train trip en route to a hospital. The records indicate that he may have picked her up in Mexico. Her feet are badly turned."

"Wait! You are talking about Randolph Bond! That was Candice's stepfather!" Chester jumped up so quickly that he knocked the chair over backwards.

"Yes. And since there were no papers to show who the

little girl was, they named her Charity Bond."

"Dr. Bond would love it! He had a big heart for the poor, the unfortunate. It seems incongruous that he would have no papers or identification on the child, though. He was normally a very regimented man, document oriented to a fault."

"It seems he would have had some sort of records."

"His wife, Hortense, made life very uncomfortable for him when he offered his services to charity cases. You say the little girl is a cripple?"

"Yes."

"Could her feet be corrected with surgery? There are so many new surgical procedures—"

"I'm sure they could. But the cost!"

"I would do the surgery without charge, Elise. In Dr. Bond's stead. If it were not for him, I wouldn't be a doctor. He was the man who financed my degree. He probably had surgery in mind when he went for the child. No doubt some poverty-stricken mother appealed to him for help and he couldn't turn her down."

"I thought most of the people from Mexico were brown-skinned. This child is almost transparent . . . and with blond curly hair."

"There are many nationalities living in Mexico."

"And she is so *smart*, Chester. She can draw anything! If she isn't an artist, I'll miss my guess. She draws pictures of objects so perfectly that *you can tell what they are*. It is going to be so much fun teaching her. She has such an eager mind!"

"You have me especially interested in your pupil, Elise. I often wondered what happened to Dr. Bond's small patient. How old did you say she is?"

"There's no birthdate given, but she was brought in five years ago and listed as 'infant' then."

"I'll be over to see your young lady tomorrow. I hope that we can help her. I'll try to work for her physically and you try to work for her mentally."

Alan slapped Chester on the shoulder. "Thanks, brother. Sometimes you are too kind for your own good. This won't get you rich."

"I keep remembering what the Master said, Alan. As you've done it unto the least of these, you've done it unto Me. Yes, Alan, this *is* what makes me rich."

CHAPTER 19

The Chase

Hortense Bond was in a dither. She blamed Chadwick Ross for not marrying Candice.

Arlene Ross defended her son. "Chadwick couldn't help it because she jumped off the train and got away from him!"

"He likely said something to rile her."

"Your Candice is spoiled, Hortense."

"And your Chadwick is a wimp!"

"I say it was Candice's fault that he went running back to Lydia."

"I say it is Chadwick's fault that Candice is at this minute stranded somewhere without her medicine!" Hortense daubed at her eyes with a perfumed handkerchief.

They fought all the way home. Barbs, accusations, and stony silences, each took a turn at making the trip wretched.

Chadwick had refused to disclose where Candice got off the train or why. When Hortense found that Candice was not in California—or wed to the banker's son—she wanted to return home immediately. But Arlene said that her husband, Roger, would be angry if she came back ahead of schedule. Hortense declared herself too upset to travel alone.

"Anyway, Candice is likely in Fort Worth now, being mollycoddled by your servants," Arlene said, trying to pacify Hortense. "Children always boomerang back like a parcel mailed with the wrong address when they run out of money. Chadwick would have returned long ago if Lydia's parents hadn't given them handouts. I'm afraid Chadwick will never divorce Lydia now. She has him tied hand and foot."

When Hortense arrived home and found that Candice had come and gone, she blew up at her employees. "While she was here, why didn't you hold her?" she stormed.

"I didn't have any handcuffs, ma'am," Harkins retorted.

"I will not tolerate back talk!"

"Pardon, madam." He made a generous bow.

Hortense turned to the cook. "Why didn't you sedate her?"

"I didn't know how much to give. If I had overdosed her, I would have been charged with murder."

"You have been dispensing pills for years, Cook. You knew exactly how much to give!"

"I do nothing without orders."

"And precious little *with* orders." She turned back to the butler. "Do you know which direction she went?"

"She said she was going to A . . . A . . . somewhere that started with an A."

"Arlington?"

"No'm."

"Arkansas?"

"No'm." He scratched his head. "Now I remember. It was Armadillo."

"Amarillo?"

"Could have been."

"Why did she go to Amarillo?"

"She said she had business there."

"Did you give her money for the fare?"

"Oh, no'm! She said she had plenty."

Then Hortense saw the Bible laid out, saw that the clipping had been discovered. She knew Candice's motive.

"Who gave Candice access to this Bible?" she thundered.

"I did," Cook responded. "I figure anybody has a right to read God's Word. Candice asked for it to do some Scripture finding."

"Candice was trying to do some *other* finding."

"How could I know that, ma'am? She asked for God's Word."

Hortense's world reeled. Her daughter had escaped and her servants had become impudent, all in a few days' time. She was losing her grasp on everything. There was also a note that Dr. Frisco had resigned the hospital and left. Anger and frustration boiled together in the caldron of her emotions.

She stalked to her room and slammed the door, planning to make some decisions that would set things back in order. It was there that she found the message Candice had left with the apologies. It lay on her pillow.

The message didn't make a grain of sense to Hortense. Candice had never made amends for any of her rebellion, and Hortense was sure there was some trick behind it. Some mockery.

"I shall go to Amarillo and find Candice and drag her home!" she shouted to the walls.

She stamped back down the staircase and threw a suitcase at Harkins, almost hitting his chest with it. "There! Help me pack!" she bellowed.

"How will you find Miss Candice?" he asked.

"I'll find her all right! I'll go to every hotel, every rooming house, and every eating place in the city," she spat. "I'll make her wish she had never tried to run away!"

However, when she got to Amarillo, she could find no trace of Candice or anything to indicate that she had ever been there. Her daughter hadn't checked into any of the housing facilities. None of the restaurant proprietors had seen her nor had any of the boutique owners.

I don't believe she came to Amarillo, Hortense decided. *She told Harkins that story to throw me off her trail. I believe she went back to Chester Harris after Chadwick Ross humiliated her by backing out on his end of the bargain. I'll find her with Chester again.*

Hortense took the train directly to Walnut Springs. Upon her arrival, she found the notice on Chester's office door. He was gone. She tried to push the door open to see if she might find some evidence that Candice had been there and was gone with him.

Old Mr. Jacobs tottered across the street to where she stood rattling the door. "Can't ye read, lady?" He squinted at her. "Dr. Harris has gone himself on a rest-up for a piece. He'll be back when he gets good and readied—and there ain't no use in you trying to break the door down like that. It's locked. If you've a stomachache, go to the drugstore over there and get you some bitters."

Hortense was indignant. "I'm looking for my daughter."

"You'd best hunt somewhere else. Have you thought about trying the merchantile shops?"

Hortense flung a look of open disgust at the old fellow. *Chester Harris closed the office when Candice came back,* she told herself. *They've gone away to be to themselves for a few days. Candice will regret this. When she comes blubbering back the next time, I'll tell her she made her bed hard and she can just sleep on it! She needn't expect a penny more of my money!*

Hortense wasn't content to return to Fort Worth without knowing where Candice was, though. Martha Harris would probably know. She could hire a hack to take her out to Martha's farm. She'd surely be able to filch some information from the old lady.

Martha handled her incredulity with remarkable aplomb. "Please do come in out of the heat, Mrs. Bond."

Hortense didn't do such a good job of hiding her own surprise. "Well, I . . . I never would have dreamed that you had such a lovely place, Mrs. Harris. I was led to believe . . . I mean, I . . . I thought . . ."

"Never mind what you thought, Mrs. Bond. It don't matter ta God er ta me either. God blessed us with this home an' ta Him an' our little bent-winged angel be th' glory. Effie—th' cripple that we wuz privileged ta raise partway—had it built 'specially fer us. But do have a sit-down an' I'll dish up supper fer you. I wuz jist fixin' to eat my evenin' meal. Since it's jist me, I eat early."

Hortense ate hungrily. "Why, I've . . . I've never tasted such *good* food, Mrs. Harris. If I ate like this all the time, I'm afraid I would lose my waistline."

"It's right outta th' garden. Them black-eyes wuz picked this mornin'. Th' new potatoes in th' Jersey cream sauce wuz dug yesterday. An' th' cornbread has off-th'-cob corn in it. Here, crumble th' cornbread in yore milk. It tastes better thataway."

Too startled to do otherwise, Hortense followed Martha's instructions. "Why it . . . it does taste better."

"Ain't nuthin' tastes good as fresh does. I can't figger why a body would like that ole artificial butter they make at th' stores what you have to put yore own colorin' into."

"You country folks have some secrets that the city people could learn from."

"We're generally healthy an' happy."

"Who is your cook, Mrs. Harris? I would be glad to pay him a very good wage if he'd come to Fort Worth to cook for my special dinners. That is, if you could spare him now and then."

Martha laughed merrily. "I ain't got no cook, Mrs. Bond. I do all my own cookin' an' cannin' an' bakin' an' cleanin' an' mendin'—" she let up for a gulp of oxygen. "An' prayin'."

"It is so . . . so quiet and peaceful here."

"Yep. An' yore welcome to stay as long as you want an' enjoy th' peaceful. But I'm calculatin' you came on fer a reason an' I'd like ta be knowin' why. City ladies don't come ta th' country jist ever'day fer th' howdy-do of it."

"I've lost Candice—"

"Oh, I know it's roughish, Mrs. Bond, on yer heart. But really she ain't lost at all."

"She isn't?"

"Oh, no! I got a glad-makin' letter from her not s'long ago lettin' me know she ain't lost at all."

"Please tell me about it."

"Why, she's in a mostest wonderful place today, Mrs. Bond! She's bound to be happy. I got a son there, too, you see an' I know how you feel about her bein' acrost th' river. An' I have a wee granddaughter there, too. They're livin' in a *mansion.*"

Hortense, thinking only earthly thoughts, had no conception of the place Martha spoke about, or that she spoke of the hereafter.

"She got her soul fixed, you see. That's th' important part. She wuz sorryin' fer her pridey ways, but I ain't one ta hold feelins when someone asks a-forgivin'."

"She left me a note, but I couldn't make sense of it."

"No, carnal minds don't."

Hortense still thought Martha referred to Candice's reunion with Chester. "I saw the note on Chester's office in town—"

"Yep. He'll be back by an' by. His patients'll jist have ta wait."

"Where did he go?"

"To Austin."

"And you are sure that my Candice is quite all right?"

"Candice is better off than you an' me."

"I've never been away from her for very long, Mrs. Harris. It's hard to give her up."

"Yes, but she wuz of th' age of accountability, Mrs. Bond. She wuz responsible fer her own soul an' she made good of it. What you got ta think on is yer own future. You ain't gettin' no younger, Mrs. Bond. Sooner er later ever' one of us has ta meet Ole Man Death an' give account of th' things done here on earth. We have more ta thank of than life; we have ta thank of death, too. Then what we

147

have here—our money er our land er our friends—won't count fer a dime. We have ta leave it all bahind an' go naked-like before God. Ifn we ain't got a coverin' of His fergivin' blood, we'll be ferever lost."

Hortense Bond sat in deep thought for a long time, realizing for the first time that she was a hollow shell of a woman, empty in spirit and soul. Martha Harris's grammar might be faulty, but her values were true. Which of the two of them was really rich?

The thought made Hortense so uncomfortable that she excused herself and returned to Fort Worth still unaware that Martha had assigned Candice to heaven with Sarah's baby and Robert.

In spite of my most noble efforts, Hortense told herself, *Candice returned to Chester Harris. All my lying and scheming has been in vain.*

After that visit with Martha Harris, Hortense was never the same. What Martha had said clung to the lining of her soul like lint, refusing to be brushed off. This uneducated country woman that she had scorned had something that she didn't have.

And she wanted that something very much.

CHAPTER 20

Journey's End

Two things hit Candice in the face when she exited the railway station in Austin: the scorching August heat and reality.

She hadn't enough money to rent a room for a week and eat, too. She had less than ten dollars in her handbag.

What a fool I've been, she berated herself, coming to grips with the taunting truth. *If I should find my child, I would have no way to feed her, keep her, or support her. I don't have a husband, a breadwinner! I have no job training. And even if I hired out to work, I couldn't leave a small child alone. What have I been thinking all these months? I wasn't thinking!*

Her heart settled down into her shoes as a great depression caught her mind in its vicelike grip. *I couldn't afford the smallest of gifts for my child: a doll, a ball, a picture book. I wouldn't be able to clothe her.*

Despair threatened to swallow her. What had Greta said? When the outlook is dark, try the up look. That was it. Candice looked up toward to sky. "God," she said aloud, "I'm Your child now, and I came here to try to find *my* child if it is Your will. I haven't much money left. Will You guide me and help me, please?"

She continued looking up as if the answer would float down from the sky.

"Did you speak to me, miss?"

Slowly, cautiously Candice turned her head as if expecting to see the Lord Himself. A shabbily dressed woman stood beside her. Her face was flushed and her hands workworn.

"I . . . I was really . . . talking to God."

"Are you needing something?"

"Well, yes. That is . . . I'm looking for a place to stay . . . at least for tonight. Would you happen to know of someone who lets out inexpensive sleeping quarters?"

The woman looked at Candice's well-designed clothing. "I have an attic room—but I'm sure it wouldn't be nice enough for you. It's hot and sometimes rats run through."

Candice shuddered, a tremor that ran from the back of her neck to her heels. But her chin jutted out. "If it is economical enough—"

"Could you pay a dollar a week? If you can't pay that much, we'll work with whatever you have. A week's rent in advance would help, but I can wait if it is necessary."

"I'd . . . I'd appreciate your room. That is, until I can find something permanent."

"Follow me."

Candice fell in step with the shuffling woman.

"I was just going home from work. It's not far from here to my place. I live on the other side of the railroad tracks and it is noisy. When the train whistles every morning, I know it's time to get up. That saves the expense of a clock."

Candice thought she had never seen such a pathetic house. The paint had worn off long ago and the steps sagged tiredly. Several boards were missing from the floor. A rub board that was propped against the wall matched the galvanized washtub with its waterline ring showing where soap had been. A makeshift clothesline stretched between the posts that held up the porch. But the inside of the house was as neat and clean as the woman could possibly make it. A Bible lay on a wobbly three-legged table. The smell of cabbage hung heavy in the air.

"If you're hungry, miss, I have some soup left over from yesterday." The woman dished up a bowl of the greasy broth for herself and Candice. Candice thought she had never tasted anything as rank, but she knew she must have nourishment, so she forced it down.

"My name is Gracie. And what shall I call you?"

"Candice."

"That's a lovely name."

"Thank you." Candice tried to smile, but her lips only managed a quiver.

"Have you traveled a far piece, Candice?"

"I came here from Abilene."

"I'm not a nosy sort and why you are here is your own business and none of mine. But if I can help you, I'll be glad to do so. I work as a scrubwoman at the children's home and I'll be gone days. Make yourself comfortable. I live alone and fend for myself. The neighbors are friendly except for one mean dog down at the end of the block."

"I . . . I'll need to get a job, too."

"You don't look hale and hearty enough to work manual labor. What jobs are you suited for?"

"I . . . I've never worked, but I'm willing to try anything. Just so it is honest work."

"You wouldn't want to hurt your back or mess up those pretty hands."

Candice studied her fingernails. "It doesn't matter," she said. "I'm stronger than I look."

"There are almost always openings over at the home. Especially in the kitchen or mopping floors or emptying slop jars. The pay isn't much. I started out at ten cents an hour back about six years ago. Now I get fifteen cents an hour. It beats doing nothing. I have no learning to do anything smarter. The little dab I get buys kerosene for my lamps and a bit of food for my stomach."

"I'd like to try the job."

When dusk came, Candice climbed the ladder to the attic where a seedy mattress sprawled on the bare floor. She lay wide-eyed and restless, staring at the bottom of the shingles. Her ears were attuned to the scurry of rats.

She had never been so discouraged. She told herself that she should have returned to Fort Worth instead of coming to a strange city. Roger Ross would have hired her on at the bank. The "seek and ye shall find" voice must have been a figment of her imagination.

In the black of that awful night, Candice wrestled with her soul and made a momentous decision. She would not try to find her child. It would be cruelly unfair to the child and to herself. If she did locate her, what could she do? Walk away and leave her again? That would cause even more trauma to a little girl who had suffered more than her share of troubles already.

She certainly would never bring a child to a place like this with rotting food and rats. No. She would have to work for many years before she could accumulate enough to make a home for her Chessica. She had put the cart before the horse; she should have earned enough to make a home for the child first. Until she could do that, she wouldn't disturb the youngster's life.

Gracie had promised to check on a job for her. She was no more "learned" than the scrubwoman. She had been sheltered and spoiled and fed with a silver spoon all her life. What good would all her ballet lessons, modeling classes, and skating trophies do her now? This was the real world.

She buried her face in the musty-smelling mattress and released an avalanche of bitter tears. She wept until her body felt drained of all resources, until she could find no more tears to shed.

When she slept, she dreamed of Chester. She fled to his arms seeking safety from a rabid rodent that chased her, trying to gnaw on her feet.

CHAPTER 21

Martha's Gift

Elise was disappointed when Chester said he was going to Brazos Point to spend the weekend with Martha. He said he would be back on Monday. Elise had planned that he escort Oneda, a nurse with whom she worked at the state school, to church.

"He probably got wind of your plans," Alan laughed. "He's gun shy."

"But Alan! He's wasting his life pining for Candice. He can't go on like this forever! There are so many lovely Christian ladies who would give an eye tooth for a thoughtful man like Chester. And Oneda is one of the nicest."

"We can't rush him, love. Harrises can be maddeningly slow, you know."

Now it was her time to laugh. "I know, Alan Harris! I waited for you for seven years!"

Oneda was at church that morning, and Elise invited her to dinner at their home. She fit right in, helping Elise with the meal and enlivening the conversation with her warm humor. She was lithe and lovely, and Alan thought she would stand beside Chester quite well.

"Who was the new woman and her daughter who sat near the back today, Alan?" Elise asked.

"The parson said her name was Gracie, but he didn't learn her daughter's name. They seemed so . . . *mismatched*. They looked nothing alike. The young lady had on an expensive dress while her mother's garments looked as though they came from the charity barrel. I didn't really get a good look at either of them; they slipped out early. The daughter kept her head bowed during most of the service."

"The woman works at the state school," Oneda offered. "She is a cleaning lady. I've passed her in the hall on several occasions."

"At any rate, I hope they will come back," finished Elise. "We don't care what their station in life is; we want them to become acquainted with our Lord."

When Oneda had gone, Elise asked, "Well, what did you think of her for Chester, Alan?"

"I think with time, Chester will grow fond of her. We must let the rose unfold as it will."

At Brazos Point, the object of their discussion went to church with Martha. The country renewed Chester's spirit, and he spent the afternoon relaxed and enjoying the time with his mother. They talked of many things. She regressed into the past then abruptly brought up Hortense Bond's recent visit.

"Hortense Bond came *here*?" Chester's voice spun upward on the last word, showing his disbelief that such a thing could happen. He hoped his mother hadn't begun to hallucinate.

"She did, indeed, Chester. An' sorrysome fer her, I wuz. Tellin' me she'd lost her daughter an' how lonely she wuz without her."

"Yes, I can see that."

"An' I'm right gladsome she came. I got ta tell her about th' letter an' how Candice had made her peace with God an' gone on ta a better place. Had it been one o' mine, that's what I'd'a wanted ta hear."

"How long did she stay?"

"Not long. 'Twas midafternoon when she came an' she dinnered with me. We had new potatoes an' fresh corn-pone. She crumbled her bread in her milk."

"Mama, you're sure—?"

"She said she'd never before ate any vittles so tasty. She wanted to borrow my cook fer her big parties. That gave me a tickle! Can't you see me in that sumptious kitchen not knowin' which spatula to spat what with?" She gave a tittering laugh. "Then we talked on awhile longer an' she up an' left in a hurry ta catch th' last train back out ta her home."

"Did she have some special purpose for coming?"

"That's what I askt her . . . an' she jist said, 'I lost my Candice.' It wuz a strange visit, but she seemed more heart-settled when she left."

"Dear Mama. You could give anybody's troubled spirit a calm-plex." He chuckled at the pun he was sure she missed.

"I told her she warn't gettin' no younger an' she needed salvation 'fore she died herself. Nobody's comin' under my roof an' goin' away a heathen!"

"Mama—you *didn't*!"

157

"Warn't I supposed to? She's a soul."

"Well, surely, but. . . ."

"I did most certainly. She jist sat still-like an' thought on what I said. My guess is that she's thankin' on it till yet in th' deep of th' night." She changed the subject as smoothly as closing a door and opening a window. "When are you comin' back home fer keeps, Chester?"

"I don't know, Mama. I'm thinking about making some major changes in my life."

"You tired o' doctorin'?"

"Yes and no," replied Chester."

"Can't be both at once."

"I'm tired of general practice. I'd like to go into another field—"

"Go into a *field*? An' be a farmer? Why, you could farm my land right here. . . ."

"No, I'm talking about another branch of the medical profession. I want to doctor children only. No adults. I want to make a study of children's diseases and cures and then later have my own clinic to treat them."

"Would there be enough children in The Springs to keep you busy?"

"No, I'd have to go to a city."

"An' yore thankin' of Austin."

"Yes. There's a great university there where I could keep abreast of new developments in the world of medicine."

"You've found a lady friend, ain't you?"

He laughed. "Elise has found one for me. She had plans for me to meet her today, but I slipped out—"

"An' here I thought you came ta see me when all th' time you wuz runnin' away—"

"I had the trip planned before I knew of Elise's cunning."

"So you'll doctor in Austin?"

"I've found a little patient at the state school who has spurred me on, strengthened my decision. She is one of the students Alan's wife will be teaching. She is clubfooted and someone should have straightened those feet long before now. At this point, it will be a long process and a lot of pain. The bones will have to be broken and her feet set in casts."

"Why didn't they do it?"

"The cost, I'm sure. She is a charity case and no one wants to put their expertise into a cause that is time consuming and expensive—and take the chance of the surgery being unsuccessful. It's not something many doctors would wish to tackle."

"An' you plan ta try it?"

"I do. And for a special reason. I have learned that this child is the one Candice's stepfather was bringing to his hospital for treatment when he died. She . . . she almost seems like a part of the family. Why, Mama, she even looks like Sarah's Tilly did when she was her age! And she has eyes like Joseph's youngest. It's a good thing you didn't see her. You would claim her as one of your own!"

"What is her name?"

"Charity."

"Well, now ain't that a sweet name?"

"She's a beautiful child. If it wasn't for her crippled feet, she would have been adopted out. Elise says she hasn't had anybody in her family visit her in all the years she has been confined there."

"Don't say it, Chester!" Martha covered her ears. "I

can't stand sayin's like that. My heart is too mushy. Ta thank th' poor darlin' has nobody!"

"I know, Mama. I feel the same way. The first time I went into her room, I wanted to pick her up in my arms and hold her forever and shield her from all life's hurts."

"How old is she?"

"It's hard to tell. She's small and frail. Her body shows about four years old, but her mind says six or seven—or older."

Martha's unfocused eyes fixed themselves on the wall, filling with tears of sympathy. "Do you thank it would be okay, Chester, if I sent little Charity a doll? Could maybe I be th' gran'ma she never had? Would God let me do that? I'd love ta send her Effie's doll with th' soft body an' th' china head."

"I'm sure she would cherish it, Mama. I didn't see a toy anywhere about."

Martha laced her fingers together in her lap. "Bad as I hate ta give you up, Chester, I know you have ta do what yer heart an' God calls fer. You have ta help these babies. It ain't too awful far ta Austin with th' modern trans-portatin' an' th' horn fer talkin'. I might even git up th' gumption ta git on that train myself an' come see that blessed little fergotten lamb you told me about."

On Monday, Chester returned to Austin, eager for his next visit to the state school. He needed to study his medical books in preparation for the surgery on the child's feet.

"How was Mama?" Alan asked.

"We can't leave Mama for a month without something wild happening, Alan," he chortled.

"What now?"

"She has been entertaining Hortense Bond at the Harris farm."

"*The* Mrs. Bond?" Alan asked incredulously.

"The same. And Mama *preached* to her. Told her to repent or perish."

"That Mama of ours has the gall of the apostle Paul!"

"Did you ever know any of her 'mama sermons' to wear lace, Alan?"

CHAPTER 22

Charity's Wish

"**D**id you see my dolly that the doctor's mother sent me, Teacher?" Charity's cherubic face lighted with joy. "It's the first doll baby I've ever had and I'll love her forever and ever. She'll always have a mommy and never cry lonesome." She hugged the doll to her chest.

A hard lump sat in Elise's throat. "I saw your baby before you did! What did you name her?"

"I haven't named her yet. I'm waiting for the right name to come by my heart, then I'll grab it. Until then I'll just call her Dolly. I may decide to leave her named Dolly forever and ever."

"Dr. Harris said his mother might come on the train to see you someday. She can be your pretend grandmother."

"I have lots of pretends. Please don't tell my secret, Teacher, but Dr. Harris is my pretend daddy. He is so *very* nice to me! Does he have some really childrens?"

"No. Dr. Harris hasn't a wife. She is in heaven. I think he would be delighted to be your pretend daddy."

"Do you think so?"

"I do. He especially likes you."

"Everything is always pretend, isn't it? I wish I could have somebody who is really mine. Did you have a real mother and a real grandmother when you were a little girl like me?"

"I had a sweet grandmother until I was grown, but my mother went on to be with Jesus when I was quite small. I hardly remember her at all."

"I sometimes wonder what it would be like to have a really really mother. But when I think on it, my heart *wants* so badly, I have to stop my mind from thinking. You understand what I mean, don't you?"

"Yes, Charity, I do."

"Sometimes I draw pictures for my really really mother. Then I throw them away before anyone sees them because they're just for her and nobody else."

"You're going to be a great artist someday. Maybe you'll even be famous."

"What's famous?"

"That's when your name is known all over the world because you draw so well, and people pay big money for your paintings."

"Where will I get the colors and the paper?"

"I'll supply them for you."

"Oh, goody! Then I can draw all I want?"

"Yes. That's a part of your schooling, and I am really really your really really teacher."

Charity giggled.

They had been in school a week now, and Charity's active mind ran ahead of the lessons. She finished her work before the hour was up, giving Elise time for visits with her.

Charity's mental perception for her age amazed Elise. Today held another surprise. "Please tell me about Jesus," the child requested. "And about His home. Your mother is there and the doctor's wife is there. The nurse told me some, but she told me not nearly enough!"

"What are you wondering about, Charity?"

"Does Jesus love cripples like me? Does He ever take *little people* to live with Him, or do they have to be grown-up?"

"Jesus loves *all* children. He said, 'Suffer the little children to come unto Me.' "

"He did?"

"He put it in His Book."

"I'm a 'suffer children.' "

Elise hugged her. "Yes, you are. And Jesus has a mansion in heaven with your name on it. Did the nurse tell you about Jesus dying on the cross for you?"

"Yes, ma'am. I wasn't worth somebody going to all that trouble for. She brought me a picture and told me about the awful nails that were put in His hands and His feet. It made me cry."

"Every scar on His body shows where He hurt to make some part of *you* feel better, Charity—your mind or your body or your heart."

Charity squeezed her eyelids closed. "I'm trying to see Jesus right now in my head," she said. "Oh, and I see them! I see the *scars!*"

Elise took her hand; it felt too hot. "If you'd like, I'll pray with you every day before I leave. And when I leave, Jesus will stay right here with you."

Charity opened her eyes slowly. "Oh, yes! I'd like that!

I think I almost saw His face, Teacher."

"It seems you have a bit of fever today. I'd better get Dr. Harris to look in on you again."

She gave a twisted smile. "It might be worth fevering to see my daddy-doctor."

"Do you still cough at night."

"Some nights are worser than others. Some nights it is hard to breathe. It seems like my wind is choking off."

"Dr. Chester thinks you may have asthma."

"What's asthma?"

"It's a lung disease. Nobody knows what causes it. With your weak lungs, he says we have to guard against pneumonia."

"What's pneumonia?"

"It's a lung infection."

"One big word makes another, doesn't it, Teacher?"

"Yes, but you can trust Dr. Harris. He is waiting for you to get to feeling better, then he'll make your feet straight and you can be adopted out."

"What will it be like? The operation, I mean."

"You won't feel anything at all while Dr. Chester is working on your feet. You will be asleep."

"And when I wake up, I can run and jump and play?"

"Not all at once. You'll have casts and plasters and then learn to walk a step at a time. Dr. Harris calls it therapy. There'll be rubs and hot soaks and lots of exercise."

"Will it hurt?"

"Sometimes it will, I'm afraid. I wouldn't be truthful if I told you that you will have no pain. You'll have to be a brave girl."

Charity bit her lip. "I know Dr. Harris wants to make me walk again, and he wants what is best for me. But there is something I would like much better."

"What is that, Charity?"

"I'd like to go see Jesus where He lives. The nurse said that nobody hurts up there in the sky ever again and no little children ever have to cry."

"That's . . . right."

"I've hurt for so long, Teacher, that I'm not sure I want any more hurts. Sometimes it hurts just to take a breath. I'm afraid that when my legs are unbent, it will be lots and lots of pain. They're *used* to being curled up, you see. The thought of the operation makes me tired. I want Jesus to hold me in His arms like I'm holding Dolly and let me rest."

"You'll feel better about it when the fever is gone. Dr. Harris will fix you up where you can walk as pertly as anybody and someone will want you in their really really home."

"But it wouldn't be my really really mother, and I'm not sure I'd like to go with somebody I don't know, Teacher."

CHAPTER 23

The Picture

Once Chester made up his mind to become a full-time pediatrician, he donated many hours of volunteer service to the state school. What better opportunity for training and experience? If the surgery on Charity was successful, word would spread and his practice would be off and running. He began looking for a building for his clinic.

He discussed his plans with Alan each evening. One day he came home chuckling. "I don't think I'll have any more problems with your boss's daughter," he told Alan. "I gave her quite a shock today."

"Helen?"

"Yes. She offered to give me a ride from town in her new roadster—and I took her up on it."

"That won't solve anything! She'll be tooling you around town from now on!"

"Oh, it's *where* I had her take me that sealed my doom."

"Let me guess. To the state school?"

"Worse than that. I promised the parson that I would make a call on the woman and her daughter who visited service the Sunday I was gone. They live in a miserable section of town down by the rail tracks. On a whim, I decided to make that call today and directed Miss Jorgensen to the location. I suppose she thought that I had taken a room there. You should have seen the look on her face when I thanked her for the ride and got out of the car. It was priceless!"

"Yes, you lost your chances with her right there, Chester." Alan kept a straight face. "Helen has to be certain of life's finery for her future. That's why she left her first husband; he didn't dole out enough money."

"She's been married?"

"Yes."

"Why didn't you tell me?"

"You didn't ask."

"I am much more comfortable among the poor than among the rich."

"It might have something to do with your raising. But tell me, did you have a good visit with the poor people you went to call on?"

"Yes, I did. Gracie, the older woman, was home alone. She said the young lady wasn't her daughter. She is a transient who recently moved here from Abilene to work at the state school."

"Did they like our church?"

"They did, and she said they would be back."

"Good. And now that you are rid of Helen," he ribbed, "Elise will want to know how you feel about Nurse Oneda."

"She's a lovely lady, Alan. A compassionate nurse. But

my heart seems . . . dead to romance. Time will change that I hope. I find myself comparing all ladies to Candice. Oneda is nothing at all like Candice—"

"I thought that's what you wanted—somebody different."

"It is, but. . . ."

How could Chester explain to Alan that he could never love another woman until Candice moved out of his thoughts. She still consumed them. This woman that Elise had introduced to him was proficient, neat, and attractive. There was nothing dislikeable about her. She would make a good companion. They had a lot in common; they had consulted on Charity's case. But Oneda didn't have the feel for the child that he had. Chester doctored the girl with his heart; Oneda nursed with her mind and her hands. The child was just another patient to Oneda, to be nurtured, cared for, and coaxed to health.

Chester found himself spending more and more time in Charity's room, at her side. He worried when her fever went up, prayed that it would subside. When she had a struggle drawing a breath, he found himself longing to breathe for her, to take her pain. "She is becoming an obsession with me," he told his brother. "I've scolded myself, lectured myself, reasoned with myself, but I can't seem to *help* myself!"

Alan realized how emotionally involved Chester had become in the case later that same week. Elise had gone to market. Chester came home from the school with a folder under his arm. He went directly to his room, and when he came out, he sat on the horsehair sofa in silence.

Alan tried to break open the conversation. "Elise says that Charity is weeks ahead of her other pupils."

Chester nodded.

"She says if the child didn't tire so easily, she would be ready for the second grade by Christmas."

Still Chester remained mute.

"Elise says that Charity loves the doll Mama sent and that she calls Mama her pretend grandmother."

Chester looked down at his feet, making no comment.

"Something is bothering you, brother," Alan said, trying to draw him out. "Like it was back at the reunion that year. Some trouble is eating at your vitals. Does it concern the child?"

Again Chester nodded.

"Are you afraid that the surgery won't be successful?"

Chester shook his head. "No, I'm not afraid of that."

"Are you concerned that she won't make it *until* the surgery, Chester?"

"I don't know." He gave a heavy sigh that seemed to issue from the bottom of his soul. "She is losing ground. I can't go ahead with the surgery as long as she is this weak. It would be too great a . . . a risk."

"I know you would like to do this operation in honor of Dr. Bond," Alan said, "and that is noble of you. He meant a lot to you and this would be a means of repaying a debt, but Dr. Bond is gone. Even if he were here, he would tell you that a doctor can only do so much. God has to do the rest. If the child isn't strong enough to undergo the treatment, you must accept it as God's will that she not have it. I'd say that you have done more than your share already. Consider the many hours you have spent. . . ."

"I'd love to give every hour of the rest of my life to her. I'd like to adopt her and show her the beauties of the outside world."

"Why, Chester, a *single* man can't adopt a child! The state wouldn't allow it. What would you do with a *girl* child?"

"She's . . . she's latched onto my heart. Those clear, trusting eyes, Alan. Today she called me Daddy-Doctor!"

"You must detach yourself, Chester. She's just another patient."

"No, she isn't just another patient. If only I had Candice. . . ."

"Even if Candice had lived and rejoined you, she might not have—"

"Candice would love Charity like a mother! I know she would! I've almost a notion to marry somebody, anybody, just to get Charity. I've never loved a child . . . like this. I love her so much I'd . . . I'd give my life for her!"

Alan considered Chester nearly irrational. "Chester! I know that you love her. Elise loves her, too. But both you and Elise have gone overboard about this one little girl. I don't doubt that Elise would take her herself, but she has just learned that we will have our own child late next spring."

"Congratulations, brother."

"I don't think Elise could handle both, as much as she would love to try. Charity needs special care."

"Yes, she does. And if the surgery should fail, she will need care from now on. But I am prepared to give it even if it takes every dime I have."

"You will have to find someone who shares your feelings."

"That will be the hard part."

"Oneda would do it."

"For *me* or for the child?"

"For you."

"That's not good enough."

"What brought on this decision about this one child? There are dozens of others in the school as precious and as needy as that one."

"Something happened today . . ." Chester bowed his head and wept openly. "Forgive me, brother. I've never been so . . . so moved by . . . by anything."

"Do you care to tell me about it?"

"She . . . little Charity . . . drew a picture during the night with the crayons and paper Elise left her. The picture—" Chester faltered and wept yet more. "It is so *profound*. I see it every time I close my eyes."

"What was it?"

"She . . . she drew the picture for her *mother* and asked me to write a caption under it. It is for the mother she never knew, Alan. She asked me not to show it to anyone. It is . . . oh, Alan! I . . . can't . . . stand . . . it!" He gave way to great sobs that shook his shoulders. "*That . . . picture!*"

CHAPTER 24

Found

Candice soon learned what a tower of strength Gracie was. This woman, who wore the heels of her shabby shoes down at an angle with the dragging of her tried feet, insisted on wrapping Candice's feet in cool towels when her ankles swelled from the long hours of standing. Gracie learned that the girl didn't like cabbage, and the soups improved. Candice's original plans to find a better place to live didn't materialize. What would she do without Gracie?

Candice wanted to visit the church again, but Gracie said that she should rest. "Sunday is the only day of the week you have off, and if you crowd that body, it will quit on you," she said. "We'll go back when your body gets broken in to your job. I'll know when it's time. Meanwhile, we will read the Bible and have our own devotions right here. God isn't confined to a church building."

They settled into a predictable routine, and Candice tried to forget the reason she had come to Austin. Her reason for being there now was simple survival. She hadn't the money to go elsewhere. She found that she preferred her present status to her life in a stupor of drugs back home. She felt her body, as well as her spirit, becoming stronger. The work was doing her good. The servants, the parties, the gaity of the past—those things seemed a world removed.

Gracie made Candice a brown muslin dress for work so that she wouldn't ruin her "fancy" clothes. The uniform made the girl look like a collapsed scarecrow. The youthful hands that were once well-lotioned became red and raw, blistered with the cleaning chemicals of the kitchen. But Candice was as proud of each paycheck as if it were a million dollars. She had earned it herself, and honestly.

Days melded into weeks with sinister sameness. Candice had little contact with anybody but Gracie. The other employees, much older than she was, made no effort to become friends. They had their own groups, their own favorite subjects.

Accustomed to samplings of their conversations, Candice thought nothing of it when she heard them discussing the sick child in Ward Seven. Some outside doctor, they said, had offered his services without charge. He had ordered a special chicken broth for the child. "He wants us to use a *whole* chicken in the soup. Why, we could feed the whole school on that much meat!" one commented.

"And she is to have some of it every two hours, not at the scheduled two meals a day," said another.

"Well, he is paying for it himself," countered a third. "He can do as he chooses."

"Here, Candice, you take this to Ward Seven," the

kitchen supervisor said, shoving the tray into Candice's hands. "It's all the way to the other end of the building, and the rest of us are tired of trotting down there."

Candice started through the building with the wonder-ful-smelling dish. She had never been to any of the children's wards; she was eager to see what they were like.

About midway there, she met a nurse. "That must be going to Charity, my little patient," the white-capped lady said. "Here, I'll take it for you, dear, and save you a few steps." Smiling, she relieved Candice of the tray.

That night, Candice told Gracie about the nurse she had met. "I think I would like to go to school and become a nurse," she said. "I . . . it was my ambition at one time, but my mother wouldn't allow it. I . . . I liked that nurse."

"That must have been Nurse Oneda," Gracie conclud-ed. "She is one of our best. She's a Christian. The children love her. I wish we had more like her."

"Do many of the children die?" Candice asked.

"Oh, a lot of them do! Too many, I think. But, of course, most aren't healthy when they are brought to the home."

"The little girl in Ward Seven,"—what is wrong with her?"

"Ward Seven." Gracie pursed her lips. "I can't remem-ber which children are in that particular ward. I've cleaned in that section. You didn't happen to hear her name, did you?"

"The nurse called her Charity."

"Oh, yes! I was working at the home when they brought Charity here. That's the little girl with the crip-pled feet. There's a long story behind her, with a lot of pages missing. A doctor who was taking her across coun-try for treatment died somewhere out west and no one was able to identify the baby—"

The world swam around Candice. She felt cold and hot and cold again. She made a gurgling sound and her food tried to come up. "I'm . . . I'm sick," she said.

Gracie ran to her side. "Why, you are as pale as the underside of a toadstool!" she fretted. "Get your head down and your feet up before you pass out on me! Breathe in short, quick gasps of air!" She ran for a thread-bare washcloth to lay across Candice's forehead. When she returned, Candice was weeping with an agony that Gracie could not understand.

"You were not born and bred for this harsh work, Candice. I knew it all the time. You don't belong in a place like the state home. I don't know who you are or what your background is, but I suspect that you are a princess in disguise. You have proved to yourself that you can make your own wage, and you know how we at the poverty level live. Now go back to the comforts of your upbringing and forget whatever you are trying to show the world before you have a complete nervous breakdown." She was kind but firm. "I'll see you back to the train and help you with your fare."

"Gracie, please don't make me go!" Candice implored pitifully. "I've just . . . I've just *found her*!"

"Found whom?"

"The little girl . . . the little sick girl in Ward Seven. She belongs to me! She is *my* baby!"

"She's talking out of her head," muttered Gracie. "Now what do I do with her? I should have sent her home before it came to this."

"No, Gracie! Please believe me. I'm very much in my right mind. The doctor who died with the baby in his arms

178

was my stepfather. His name was Randolph Bond. My little girl was born in Arizona, and he was taking her back to Fort Worth to our hospital when he had his heart attack. My mother—she didn't want the care or expense of the baby—wouldn't even tell me where my stepfather died. I've been searching . . . for my baby." A panic pinched her sentence into fragments. She put her face down to her lap. "Oh, please . . . please believe—"

"There, there, little mother. I believe you." She crooned a mixture of concern and comfort. "Your story connects. They called her Baby Bond when she was brought in no bigger than a drowned rat! The nurses named her Charity."

"Her name is Chessica, for her daddy. His name was Chester."

"He's dead?"

"No he . . . He is remarried. He doesn't know about her."

"The poor lamb didn't get much medical treatment for all these years, but she has a jim-dandy doctor on her case now. He has the nurses goose stepping to his orders. They say he plans to do surgery on her feet and straighten them. His name is Dr. Harris."

"Dr. . . . *who*?" Another wave of sickness hit Candice in the pit of her stomach.

"Harris. He came in one day while I was cleaning the ward. I've never seen a doctor so gentle with a patient. He brought her a doll."

"You . . . you don't know his first name?"

"No, I never heard it. He's not a staff doctor. He's a volunteer. I've never seen a doctor take so much interest in one crippled child, though."

"Is . . . is the child's mind all right?"

"Oh, she is as sharp as a tack! I've been in when her teacher was schooling her. She already knows her letters. The teacher's name is *Mrs.* Harris."

"Mrs. Harris? The doctor's *wife*?"

"I never asked, but I would suppose so. They seem chummy enough, but still professional. They do good teamwork."

"What does she look like, Gracie? I want to recognize her when I see her."

"Mrs. Harris?"

"No, Chessica. I mean Charity."

"She has big pretty eyes, the same color as yours, and gold hair that is as fine as spun silk with curls that make themselves into ringlets. She is a *beautiful* child, prettier than a picture."

Candice, caught up in the description, smiled a dreamy smile. All the sickness went away.

"I'll be late coming home tomorrow, Gracie, so don't worry about me. When I get off work, I am going to Ward Seven to meet my little girl. God wouldn't have let me find out about her if He didn't want me to see her. Please say a prayer for me."

CHAPTER 25

A Really Really Mother

The day seemed an eternity cut up into individual segments of endless hours. Candice couldn't keep her mind on her work and was reprimanded by her supervisor several times for her carelessness. She spilled some milk, forgot to turn off a burner, and dropped a potato. "I'll have to let you go if you can't do better than this, Candice Sharp," her boss said harshly.

Candice felt a panic in her throat. "I'm . . . I'm sorry, ma'am. I will try to be more careful." And try she did. She couldn't afford to lose her job now that she had found her child! She would want to be right here year in and year out so that she could visit every day and be near Chessica.

There were probably many Dr. Harrises, but if, by some fluke of bad luck, this one turned out to be Chester, she wouldn't bother his new life. She would visit only when he was not there, and neither he nor the child would ever know. . . .

The supervisor held her over to redo some of the pots

and pans that she had not cleaned thoroughly. It seemed a thousand weary hours before she was able to hang up her apron and leave the kitchen. It was six o'clock and already getting dark outside before she got to Ward Seven.

Charity was asleep with her doll cradled in her arms. Candice stopped in the doorway, her pulse racing. Happy tears filled her eyes. Here was her child! There was no mistaking the identity. She was a miniature of Chester and herself! Anyone in the world should be able to tell to whom she belonged.

She stood over the child, drinking in every detail of her pixy face, her regal head. Then she reached out shyly and touched her small hand. *Chessica. You are a part of me.* She bent to kiss her head and a tear fell into the tangle of blond curls. She became braver.

"Chessica," she whispered, "Mommy is here. Mommy found you. . . ."

Charity stirred and opened her eyes. "I know," she smiled, a tiny smile that made Candice's heart twist and jump. "I dreamed you came. That was Jesus telling me you would." She reached out her arms, and Candice enfolded her in a long embrace.

"Will you take me home with you, Mommy?"

"Someday I will. Until then, I will spend every minute that I can with you. We'll play games and read books and make plans—"

"Now I have a really really mother."

"And I have a really really beautiful little girl. And do you know what her really really name is?"

"Yes, her name is Charity."

"Her mother named her Chessica."

Charity clapped her hands together. "I like my really really name!"

Just then, Charity went into a terrible spasm of coughing and almost lost her breath. Her chest rattled with a deep, wheezing noise. It frightened Candice.

"Are you all right, sweetheart?"

"Dr. Harris says I have asthma. He's my da—doctor. He's going to make my feet straight, but it really doesn't matter, does it? A really really mother likes crooked feet, too."

"A really really mother loves her child just the way she is, Chessica. We will find a way, you and I, to be together forever no matter what."

"God will find a way."

When Candice left, her feet scarcely touched the ground all the way to Gracie's tumble-down shack. She had never been so happy, felt so light. She counted the hours, the minutes, and the seconds until she could return to Ward Seven. What God had for the future, she didn't know, but for today—just for today—her joy was complete.

She told Gracie about the day, the meeting. "It was so hard to leave her," Candice said. "She begged to come home with me."

"We will bring her here, Candice," Gracie decided. "You can stay at home with her and take in ironings for the rich folks, and I will keep working at the home. We will manage."

"Not yet." Candice spread out her hands. "As much as I would love to have her here now, we must keep our secret until the doctor gets her feet repaired, Gracie. Neither you nor I will ever have enough money for the surgery. The doctor might back out if he learns about our plans to remove her from the school."

"That is wise thinking, Candice. We'll bide our time."

"I can spend evenings and all day Sunday with her. And oh, Gracie, she loved her name! She called it her 'really really' name."

The next day when Chester put the stethoscope on Charity's chest and then on her back, he frowned. Elise was there giving a lesson; he called her out of the room. "I don't like what I hear, Elise. I'm afraid we're in trouble. Pneumonia can take a child down fast."

"I know, Chester. I've been worried for days about the chronic fever."

"Daddy-Doctor . . ."

"She's calling you, Chester."

Chester dashed into the room and patted Charity's cheek. "What do you want, princess?"

"My mother came to see me. My really really mother."

"When, Charity?"

"I don't remember. But she came."

"In a dream, Chester," furnished Elise.

"No, not in a dream, Teacher. She really really came. My really really name isn't Charity. It is Chessica."

"Why, what an unusual name!" Elise said. "I've never heard it before. Have you Chester?"

Chester's jaw twitched. "I've only heard it once. That's what . . . that's what Candice planned to name the little girl we never had. Elise, I feel so . . . so strange about everything. It is as if Candice is looking down from the sky or . . . or standing somewhere close by urging me to take care of this child in the place of the one we never had. Am I making sense, or am I losing my mind?"

184

"Maybe a little of both," Elise said.

"And Daddy-Doctor—"

"Yes, precious?"

"You will give my really really mother our secret picture, won't you? Now I know that I drew it *just right* for her. . . ."

CHAPTER 26

Two Scars Against One

Candice walked alone in the black darkness that once would have terrified her. Her own safety no longer mattered. A few minutes longer in the ward with Charity was worth any sacrifice she was called upon to make. She hugged every moment with the child to herself.

Life had changed since she found her daughter. The past, present, and future met as friends in the parlor of her soul, understanding and pardoning each other. Only the terrible scar remained on her heart, a scar that would torment her forever.

Charity's fever had been especially high this evening. And she had said some disturbing things. "I don't want to leave you, my really really mother," the child said, "but Jesus is calling for me to come home. Do you mind?"

"When the doctor gets your feet well, we will move you to Gracie's, Chessica. You won't have to leave Mommy ever again."

"But I'll already be moved."

Candice "kept the sayings in her heart" when she went to sleep that night, and sometime in the middle of the uneasy darkness, she awoke with a start. She thought she heard Charity call her name. She threw on her uniform and ran all the way to the state home. The guard recognized her as an employee and nodded as she passed.

Charity's breathing was labored and ragged. She had slipped into a state of semiconsciousness. Candice pulled a chair to the bedside and held the child's hand, praying tearful prayers, aware that Charity was slipping away.

The little girl rallied once, trying to focus her vision. She moved her mouth.

"What, my lamb?"

"Daddy . . . picture. . . ."

"No, sweetie, Mommy doesn't have a picture of your daddy."

Charity shook her head, "*Picture. . . .*"

"Your daddy is a prince of a man. He is a doctor."

A wisp of a smile crossed the waxen features. "Daddy-Doctor."

She said no more. The rise and fall of her small chest slowed. Then it stopped.

Candice laid her head on the lifeless little body. "Thank You, God . . . that You let me find her before . . . before You took her home."

She should notify the night nurse, who would call the coroner. But she wanted to stay a while longer, just she and her Chessica. The angels were nearby. It was peaceful.

Candice fell asleep.

That's where Chester found her when he came to check on Charity the next morning. At first, he thought he was seeing an apparition. *Two corpses.*

"It . . . it can't be! Oh, God," he cried, leaning against the wall for support. "My wife and my baby! Why couldn't I see it? How could I have been so blind? And my baby . . . she *knew.* . . ."

How cruel the years had been to Candice! Her hands, once white and pampered, were chapped and rough, her face weathered. No paint colored her lips, and no rouge tinted her cheeks. The old brown dress didn't fit her anywhere. But he thought her more beautiful than she had ever been, and his heart burned with pride as he looked at her. Her copper-tipped lashes still held tiny prisms that testified of her sorrow.

How she must have loved their child! And how much she had suffered!

How scarred her heart must have been! If only he could have known. . . .

Candice drew a long, gasping breath, and Chester realized that he had been holding his. In an instant he was beside her, calling her name. "*Candice.*"

She awoke, caught in a cobweb of grief and confusion. "Yes?" She turned her head from side to side.

When she saw him, she pulled away in a belated reflex of alarm. "I'm—I'm sorry. I didn't mean to be here when you came. . . ."

"It's all right."

"She's gone . . . my little Chessica is gone!"

"She is with Jesus, Candice."

"Yes. And I'll . . . I'll go now."

"Please don't!"

"I . . . I must."

"Where are you going?"

189

"To . . . to Gracie's house. The . . . the state will take care of her . . . her body, won't they? I . . . I haven't the . . . the means. Forgive me. I . . . I won't ever bother you again."

"I will take care of everything, Candice. And if you must go, please let me take you."

"Please, no. Mrs. Harris might not . . . understand."

"You mean Elise?"

"I don't know her name. Your . . . your new wife."

"My *wife*? Candice, darling, you are the only wife I have ever had or ever want! I . . . I thought you were dead."

"You're not . . . married again?"

"No more than you are dead."

"You know, don't you? This was our little girl, yours and mine."

"Yes, and I thank you for her, Candice. I wish we might have enjoyed her together, but God knows what is best. She showed me what God wanted me to do with my life." *What a bittersweet morning!* He'd lost; he'd gained.

"I will miss our angel-child." Candice stroked Charity's hair. "But she brought me a few days of happiness—"

"And she brought us together again."

"Yes, oh yes!"

Chester smothered her words with tender kisses. Holding her close, he whispered, "Our daughter left something for her mother. Something special."

"She did?"

"Yes. She was a very talented child, a wonderful artist. She drew a picture for you and asked me to write a note beneath it for you."

"She tried to tell me about the picture with her last

words. I understand now! She was telling me that you had it!"

He slipped the crayoned painting from his case. "The message she left will sustain you for as long as you live, Candice. It is profound. Chessica Harris had an insight that few adults are granted."

Chester handed the child's last masterpiece to Candice. Through a curtain of tears, she studied it. Two nail-scarred hands reached up to comfort a mother-heart that had a jagged scar across it. Underneath, she had "Daddy-Doctor" inscribe these words: *Two Scars Against One.*